IN SEARCH OF A WITCH'S SOUL

D. LIEBER

D1564024

Copyright © 2018 by D. Lieber. Published by Ink & Magick.

First paperback edition March 2019

Cover Design and Layout by Bryan Donihue, Section 28 Publishing

Edited by Cover to Cover Editing

ISBN 978-1-7328323-0-5

ACKNOWLEDGMENTS

A special thanks to John, Mom, Dad, Aunt Debbie, Bryan, Amy, Megan, Laura, Karissa, Michelle, Mary, Kyla, Joyce, and Chris for all your help and staying patient while I badger you with questions.

PROLOGUE

LEO

I blindly stuffed clothes in a suitcase in my haste to take off.

Fjolnir...

Every time I thought his name, a feverish desire to see him overcame my senses.

I looked around my bedroom, which was disheveled from packing, to see if I'd forgotten anything.

My eyes found a framed photograph of Rose. Her signature in the corner elegantly declared her love for me.

I paused, dazed, and tried to remember what I'd been doing. As I struggled to clear my mind, a sweet fog settled in. *Fjolnir...*

"Ah," I sighed, recalling my purpose. Rose didn't seem so airtight when I saw her again. I turned the photograph face down and rushed toward the true object of my passion. My thirsty soul could only be quenched by his touch.

I paused only briefly by the entryway mirror to

straighten my cream-colored, polka dot bowtie and put on my porkpie hat. I barely remembered to lock the door to my brownstone as I sped toward the waiting motorcar. The three-quarters moon nagged me as if I was forgetting something.

All other thoughts left when I saw the passenger door open to reveal my love. He smiled seductively, and his eyes beckoned under the brim of his fedora.

"Get in," his caramel voice invited.

I scrambled into the passenger seat, slamming the door behind me. In my enthusiasm, I threw myself toward him.

"Be gentle," he soothed, stopping my approach with a hand on my chest.

He tilted his hat up with a flick of his index finger. Gently gripping my chin, he slowly leaned in. My breath hitched in anticipation. His lips burned mine like a brand, and I moaned with unsatisfied need. I tried to push and take more, but his hand on my chest remained immovable.

His smile as he pulled away was maddening. "I have a big surprise planned for you."

I squirmed in eager anticipation.

He reached into his pocket and pulled out a strip of black cloth. This time, his smile was mischievous. I liked that, too.

"Will you let me put this blindfold on you, Leo?" he asked in an enticing tone.

A small jolt of fear made me shiver. He met my eyes with his hypnotic blue abyss.

"Get a wiggle on," he urged. "I want it to be a surprise."

Wanting to please him, I nodded and let him put it on me. My vision taken, I could still feel the air move as he waved his hand in front of me.

But I didn't expect his lips on my ear as he whispered, "It'll be more fun this way."

My heart leapt in response, and I took pleasure in the wait for him to touch me again.

It's difficult to say for how long we drove since I burned with anticipation. I did notice the sounds of the city quiet, and the road became bumpier.

When we finally came to a stop, Fjolnir gently removed my blindfold. I blinked hard a few times so my vision could adjust. His eyes sparkled with excitement.

"Follow me," he urged in a hushed tone.

The gravel of the country drive crunched beneath our shoes. In the bright light of the moon, I saw a small farm-house and a large, red barn ahead. Our frosted breath shimmered like puffs of pixie dust as we exhaled into the winter night.

The closer we got, the more eager Fjolnir became. He grabbed my hand and pulled me toward the one-story home. We entered through a side door into a small, ordi-nary kitchen.

Fjolnir flitted around, going to the cupboard then the icebox, as I stood in the doorway.

"Come in," he invited, handing me a glass of sparkling wine.

He looked pleased with himself, so I couldn't help but smile in return.

He held up his glass. "To love, the best magic there is."

"To love," I replied, and we both downed our drinks.

As I set my glass on the counter, I took a step toward Fjolnir. His proximity in the small space was driving me mad. *I can't wait anymore.*

The moonlight shone through the window, making Fjolnir's blond hair white. His blue eyes were as bright as

Venus. I halted my approach to drink in his ethereal beauty.

"Before I make your desires reality, I have something to show you. Will you follow me to the barn?"

I nodded, reining in my need as it struggled to run wild. *I'll follow you anywhere.*

The night air was cold but did nothing to shrink my libido.

Fjolnir unhitched the barn door and gestured for me to enter first.

An army of candles lit the large room, illuminating an altar at the center of a partial magic circle painted in black.

As I squinted my maladjusted eyes to read the symbols of the circle to determine its purpose, the barn door slid closed behind us. I spun around at the sound. Another witch stood by the door. His black hair shined like sleek feathers in the candlelight.

My mind went fuzzy, and I tried to blink away my blurring vision. "Who's that?" I demanded of Fjolnir, upset our time alone had been interrupted.

Fjolnir turned a too innocent face toward me. "Who? Him? He's a friend."

Before I could express my feeling of betrayal, my knees wobbled and everything went black.

ONE

ANNA

The joint was dimly lit but lively. Ciggy and incense smoke wafted through the air as sparkling threads of magic emanated from the musicians on the small stage. Revelers danced on the crowded floor, celebrating the end of the war. The prohibition on magic didn't go into effect until January, and everyone was trying to experience it while they still could.

I gazed longingly at the couples button shining. My eyes shifted to my own fella.

Jack warned me that returning doughboys would be different, but Cy seems even more changed than the rest.

I watched Cy throw back another shot. His eyes already swam with drink. His pal Victor slapped him on the shoulder with an affectionate grin.

"I'll get you another," Victor offered then swanned to the bar like he was skating on ice.

I leaned in toward Cy and whispered, "I thought it was only the two of us tonight?"

He shrugged and wouldn't meet my eyes. Cy was never so evasive.

"Look, I get it. You became friends over there. You protected each other and kept each other alive. I'm grateful to him. Believe me. But Cy, I haven't been alone with you since you've been home." I pleaded for his understanding and covered his hand with mine.

He snatched his hand away, getting into a lather. "You think you understand, Caill? You can't possibly imagine what we've seen!"

And there it is. Jack's warnings hadn't prepared me for how I felt when Cy yelled or pulled away.

"What's eating you?" Victor asked, returning to the table.

"Nothing," Cy grunted and downed the hooch Victor had handed him.

My frustration reached its limit. "You could've told me you were bringing someone at least. I wouldn't have told Jack he couldn't come."

Cy squinted accusingly. "If I would've died over there, you'd be with that coward now. Wouldn't you?"

I flinched as if he'd slapped me. "Cy, that's unfair. You know Jack's parents wouldn't give him permission to enlist."

"Your only reaction is to defend him? You don't deny you'd be with him?"

Before I could respond, Cy stood from the table and leaned toward me. "I'll show that weasel not to go after what's mine." His tone trailed down my spine like an icy finger.

"Cy, stop. You, Jack, and I have been friends since we were children. Are you really going to throw that away on baseless jealousy?"

"You know what? You aren't even worth it," he spat.

The finality of his tone made my nose burn and my eyes water. *What is happening?*

I never cried around Cy. He always saw me as an equal, so I tried to be tough like him. But this was too much to keep in.

I waited for him to take back his hurtful words as silent tears betrayed my weakness.

His drunken eyes softened with regret.

"Let's blow, Vic," he said, grabbing his jacket. Victor followed him out the door, and I sat shocked and alone.

I didn't hear the din of the crowd around me. I didn't hear the jazz singer on stage wailing for her lost love, but my heart felt her words as the woeful melody seeped into me.

At some point, a waitress tapped me on the shoulder. "You need help gettin' home, Hon?"

The noise of the club suddenly came crashing down around me. My senses overwhelmed, I struggled to formulate what I needed to do. I licked my tear-swollen lips. "May I use your telephone?"

She nodded, and we wound through the blur of full tables to the bar.

She pointed to the candlestick telephone, and I picked up the receiver. "Operator?" I called into the mouthpiece. "Connect me with Redwood 8-4653."

"One moment please," a dissonantly chipper woman responded.

"Hello?" Jack's voice asked after a few minutes.

"Jack—" I started.

"Anna? What's wrong?" Though I tried to keep my voice from trembling, he immediately knew I was upset.

"Cy—"

"Where are you?"

"Zelda's."

"I'll be there in fifteen minutes. Just stay there."

I heard a click as he hung up.

I tried to keep myself from spiraling while I waited for Jack. The seconds ticked slowly on, but I clung to the knowledge that he was coming. Always true to his word, Jack rushed in with two minutes to spare. His sharp aquamarine eyes raked my face as he rested his hands on my shoulders. "What happened?"

"Will you just take me home?" I whispered.

Not one to push, Jack nodded and helped me into my jacket.

By the next morning, I'd convinced myself Cy and I would work things out. Though we'd never fought like that before, I knew we were goofy for each other. Still, I couldn't bring myself to eat at breakfast. I twirled my spoon and watched out the window of our dining room. The sun and the autumn leaves were far too cheerful for my present state of mind, and I looked down at the delicate lace tablecloth in disgust.

By some grace, Dad and Aunt Vi hadn't noticed my mood and were discussing the labor strikes that were no doubt in the morning paper. It took me a few minutes to recognize the silence when they'd stopped talking. They both stared at the paper in mute horror.

"What is it?" I moved to read over Dad's shoulder.

"Don't—"

It was too late.

DOUGHBOYS SURVIVE TRENCHES ONLY TO PERISH IN QUARRY AT HOME

Photographs of a wrecked motorcar at the bottom of a quarry weren't as horrifying as the adjacent photograph of Cy in his Army uniform.

"What? No…"

"No," I gasped myself awake.

My heart hammered in my chest. Sighing, I wiped the sweat from my face and let the old wound settle back into its place in my soul. It took longer than usual to get back to equilibrium. The memory I'd just relived was the most painful I'd ever had. On the other hand, the memory I'd experienced the day before was of the night Cy and I had first made love. *This is always the worst part of the Living Memory spell. But whatever nightmarish memories I have to relive, it's worth it for the happy ones.*

Early morning sunlight struggled through my grimy office window. The light illuminated the scattered papers on my solid desk. I sat up from the couch at the center of the room. A cup of cold coffee mocked me from the short table that separated me from two leather armchairs. I'd been so tired the night before that I couldn't even fortify myself to get my paperwork done.

The clock above the entrance door told me my secretary, Maggie, wouldn't be in for a few hours. My stomach grumbled. *I haven't eaten since yesterday afternoon.* I decided to eat breakfast at a nearby diner. After pulling fresh clothes from the wardrobe, I went to the bathroom to clean up.

TWO

After I was refreshed, I braced myself and plastered on the smile I always wore at home, knowing he would hear my frown.

Dad never made a fuss about me not coming home as long as I checked in every forty-eight hours, and I never returned until Living Memory's side effects wore off. I rang the house from my office telephone.

"Dad? I'm at the office."

"Anna! Very good, my girl. I knew you wouldn't fail your old Dad. Vi was fretting as if we'd never see you again."

"You're not that old, Dad."

His chuckle turned into a coughing fit, and I held my breath until it subsided.

"How're you feeling?"

"Oh fine, fine."

I bit my lip at his carefree tone. "Dad, why don't you let me bring a healer? I have contacts in the magical community."

He scoffed. "What's a healer going to do that a doctor can't?"

"Dad, they're magic. I've heard they have a treatment for—"

"Those charlatans aren't coming anywhere near me. They couldn't even save your mother."

I bit my lip. *How many times have I told him that even magic can't save someone who has lost too much blood in childbirth?* I sighed. "I'm sorry I upset you. I'm just worried."

"I know you are, my girl. But take heart, your old Dad will be kicking for a while yet."

I hummed my acknowledgment.

"Will you be coming home tonight?"

"Probably. I'm meeting Jack for dinner."

"Ah. Well, tell Jackie Boy not to be a stranger. It's been a while since I've seen him."

"I will. I love you, Dad."

"I love you too, my girl."

I bundled in my hat and coat and left my office. The reception room's only source of light was the semicircle window. It barely illuminated the desk at the center of the room where Maggie usually worked. I shivered, vowing to light the stove before Maggie came in. Along with a desk chair and a client chair, the only other furniture in the room was a coatrack near the entrance and file cabinets, which guarded Maggie's back.

Shuffling outside the frosted-glass front entrance made me try to squint past the backward letters that declared my name and profession. They were blacked out as a shadow approached.

I reached for the revolver Dad had given me when I'd taken over the business. The weight of it in my hand was reassuring.

I held it at the ready but dropped it low near the hem

of my knee-length skirt. With my free hand, I unlocked the door and cracked it.

"Ms. Caill?" a silky male voice asked. "I apologize for the early hour, but are you available now? I'd like to hire you."

I sighed in relief and put my gun back in my handbag.

"Of course, come in."

I turned on the overhead light and moved farther into the room so he could enter.

Hat in hand, he sauntered in. He was like amber bourbon, warm and soothing to look at, but his demeanor was as cool as the ice that clinks in the smooth glass. I knew a taste of him would burn all the way down. His golden-brown hair was disheveled as if he'd been worrying it, but his light, brown eyes were unruffled.

I felt my face heat as my unexpected desire shamed me. He didn't give any indication he'd noticed either my reaction to him or my embarrassment.

"Won't you please come into my office, Mr…"

"Jesse Hunt."

He followed me into the next room, and I motioned for him to take a seat. He made himself comfortable on the couch, where I had so recently been sleeping.

"How may I help you, Mr. Hunt?" I encouraged, sitting across from him.

"I was referred to you by Lillian. She said you help those in the magical community."

I nodded. My Living Memory dealer often sent clients my way.

I waited for him to continue, taking the opportunity to study his face. A war of emotions brewed within me.

"My friend is missing. He was supposed to meet me last night, but he never showed. I called him and visited his home, but there was no answer. I contacted everyone I could think of who might know where he is but came up empty. I even went to the three nearest hospitals, and he wasn't there."

I tried to sound soothing while not dismissing his concerns. "Are you sure your friend didn't just stay the night somewhere?"

He shook his head. "No, Leo doesn't even like to be late. He would've called to cancel if he couldn't make it."

"Where and when were you supposed to meet?"

"He said he had something to discuss with me before our full moon ritual in a few days. We were to meet at The Black Moon at eight."

"Do you know where he was earlier in the day?"

"He told me he was meeting someone, but he didn't say whom. Honestly, he's been rather erratic lately. I know that lends credence to the idea that he forgot to call me, but I feel something's wrong."

"How has he been erratic?"

He paused as if he had to order his thoughts. I sat up straight when I realized I'd been leaning toward him, and I used the silent break to berate myself for being drawn to him.

"Sometimes he seems like he's in a giddy fog like he's daydreaming. Other times, he seems balled up and almost frightened, but he won't tell me what about."

I listened as closely as I could, but my unexpected reaction to him, and the after effects of the particularly strong dose of Living Memory I'd taken the day prior, left me feeling the beginnings of the screaming meemies.

"All right, Mr. Hunt. I have a few things to do this morning. Why don't we meet at your friend's house around noon?" *I need another fix before I look anything over, or I won't be able to concentrate. And,* I took Jesse Hunt in again, *I need to see Cy.*

He seemed to hesitate.

"I know you're worried, but your friend is probably fine. It's only been a few hours since he didn't show. Give him time to come home."

I handed him a piece of paper and a pen from my desk. "Write down his name and address."

He complied with my instructions and handed me the paper.

"There's a diner nearby if you'd like to fortify yourself with a cup of joe. I imagine you might need it after the night you've had."

"Thank you, Ms. Caill. I trust you'll find Leo."

"You can count on me."

He gave me a smile like a kick in the chest and put on his hat to leave.

As I watched him hoof out of my office, I damned fashion designers everywhere for making the long suit jacket popular. Then, I scowled at myself. *What has gotten into me?*

THREE

I left Maggie a note and grabbed a pastry from a nearby bakery on the way to Starlight Avenue.

People crowded the streets on their routes to work. Huddled in their dark winter coats with their hatted heads tucked in to keep their necks warm, they looked like a waddle of penguins as they shuffled along. The enjoyable crisp air of autumn had given way to the blades of winter wind. It hadn't yet snowed, but I looked hopefully at the clouds overhead.

I loved the first snowfall. Everything was so fresh, and the pure white flakes covered the filthy, scarred face of the city. I knew the grime was still there, but it was nice to pretend. My one vain belief in life was that if you pretended long enough, you could convince even yourself.

Holiday decorations already sparkled in the shop windows though Thanksgiving had only been the week before. Even in light of that, everyone seemed more excited than usual. I stopped at a newsstand.

"What's happening, Mac?" I asked the man next to a shrinking stack of newspapers.

"Ford released the new Model A. Want to see the photographs?" He held out a paper to me.

"No, thanks."

I continued down Huntington Street until I hit Wilbur Avenue. As expected, the squawkers were gathered on the corner. Their leader stood on a soapbox, preaching to anyone who'd listen.

"The Devil's got his claws in you, but you don't *have* to be a witch. Come toward the light and let Jesus Christ save you. This magic you practice corrupts God's plan for you. It tempts you away from his path…"

The tirade went on as usual, and I tried to pass as quickly as I could. *They're born witches, you imbeciles. You already got magic banned for humans. What more could you possibly want?*

I knew I shouldn't let them irritate me every time I saw them, but then I thought of how long witches had lived in the shadows and how far we'd thought society had come. Of course, while the revelation that magic exists had delighted many, others quaked in fear and felt the need to squash what they didn't understand and could never possess.

After turning on Wilbur Avenue, I went into a large house with an unimposing sign in the window, which read, "Clinic for Internal Medicine."

The reception area was like any other physician's home. There were uncomfortable looking chairs for waiting clients and a commanding nurse, who doubled as a secretary. The white walls were severe against the dark, hardwood floor.

The clinic couldn't have been open for long because there was only one patient waiting, a woman round with child.

My heels clicked on the floor as I ankled to the nurse's desk.

"I'm here to see Dr. Zodiac."

Though the nurse had seen me many times, including the day prior, she stared at me hard to determine my purpose. Finally, she nodded. "The doctor is available at the moment. Go to the door at the end of the hall."

I thanked her and went through the closed door behind her. I passed a legitimate exam and surgery room before I reached the end. After entering an inconspicuous door, I climbed down a flight of stairs, dimly lit by a naked bulb overhead. A thick carpet muffled the sound of my descent.

When I reached the solid, iron door at the bottom, I knocked in three groups of three. A slot at eye level slid open.

"The archer can never shoot the flame because it's within him," I whispered to the eyes.

Metal scraped, and the door opened. I entered the tunnel of Starlight Avenue. Though the tunnel was raw earth, it was smooth and well-lit by electric lights every few feet. At various points, it branched off into other tunnels, all of which led to different destinations that could fulfill any magical need.

After the guard had closed and locked the door behind me, he looked down his crooked nose at me in expectation.

"I need to see Lillian," I told him.

He closed his dark eyes and cupped his hands. As he spoke the magic words, a violet will-o'-the-wisp formed in his palms. He set it free as if it were a bird, and I followed it as it floated toward Lillian's.

Though the tunnels seemed easy enough for those who knew the way, they were in fact enchanted. Visitors without a guide, especially humans like me, would be lost and trapped until the witches saw fit to release them from the enchantment.

I followed my violet guide to a familiar door, where it disappeared. Pressing my palm to the cream-colored wood, I waited. Once the door recognized me as a friend, it unlocked with a click. Chimes tinkled as I entered the staircase that led to Lillian's sitting room.

Hers was a quaint little house, which served as an office and home. The atmosphere was always soothing with soft candlelight and plush seating. I sat in a nearby chair and waited for Lillian to appear.

Every time I visited, I was struck with the thought that Lillian must only allow clients and friends to call because there's really no hiding that she's a witch.

Even though prohibition only banned witches from practicing magic in public and around humans, most at least attempted to make the public rooms of their homes average in appearance. But that was not Lillian's way. She'd been raised to fear and hide from humans like all the witches before her. Lillian came of age when the magical community revealed itself to the humans in 1888. She'd reveled in her newfound freedom, and she wasn't going to give it up for a bunch of closed-minded religious radicals who happened to have the government's backing.

The wallpaper in her house seemed to glimmer as if reflecting all the magic it had seen over the years. Crystals glowed faintly on almost every surface, and there were bookshelves full of spells, recipes, and stories about the history of witchcraft.

If all that wasn't enough to give her away, the smell was. The heady scent of magic-enhancing incense wafted through the house even when it wasn't burning. There was no mistaking that potent aroma. After prohibition, it was illegal to make, sell, or transport. Naturally, it was in high demand.

Lillian descended the stairs to the sitting room. She'd laughed in the face of modern fashion, preferring long, flowing dresses with wide sleeves to the popular knee-high skirts and shoulder-revealing blouses. She even kept her dark, curly hair long—while I preferred my chestnut, wavy hair short, like most modern women.

She smiled as I stood to meet her.

"Anna, I had a feeling I'd see you sometime today, though you usually wait a few days between sessions."

"Well, I have to be in peak condition for that case you sent me. Thanks for that. And yesterday's memory was one I had a particularly strong desire to relive."

She nodded. "Therefore, your after-effects and cravings are stronger. I did warn you."

"I know, but I really needed to feel him yesterday."

She pursed her lips in mild disapproval. "And today?"

"Just enough to get me in my right mind to examine a potential crime scene."

"May I ask why Jesse wanted to hire you?"

"You know I can't discuss that if he didn't tell you."

She pouted.

"On that note, what do you know about him?"

Her eyes lit up with mischief. "Why? Are you *interested?*"

"I'm interested." *Because knowing about my client could help my investigation.*

She grinned suggestively. "I knew you would be."

"So what can you tell me about him?" I asked, using her misunderstanding to my benefit.

She crossed her arms, thinking. "Not a whole lot, I'm afraid. As far as I know, he's only been around for about a year. I don't think he's from one of the old covens. But he must have some connections because he and Leo became inseparable so quickly. He even joined Leo's coven."

Leo? The friend Jesse hired me to find. "Who's Leo?" I asked nonchalantly.

"Leo is the high priest of an ancient coven. He's the youngest high priest that coven has ever had. Normally, the leader of a coven would never name such a young successor. It created quite a stir."

"Why was he chosen then?"

She crooked her mouth in thought. "Well, they say he has a lot of potential. Of course being so young, it's mostly unrealized. I think it's because there was so much corruption and greed among the higher ranks that the high priestess chose Leo for his fairness. He's still young, but he possesses a strong moral compass. Besides, the priestess named an older member, who had no desire to lead, to help Leo as his advisor. I've heard he's progressing quickly, but that's probably because he has access to the coven's book of shadows."

"What's a book of shadows?"

Her eyes widened a little, and she bit her lip like she'd said an earful.

It seems that's all I'm going to get. She may be a gossip, but Lillian has never given away sensitive information on the magical community to a human. It's not like we're friends.

"You came here for a Living Memory spell. Didn't you? Please follow me to a guest room."

FOUR

My pulse quickened at the prospect of seeing Cy. I tried to keep my pace steady as I followed Lillian to the door under the stairs. The broom closet looked standard as far as broom closets are concerned. There were a few crates stacked neatly along the left wall, and a broom leaned, bristles up, against the bare wallboards. The naked bulb overhead swung from being pulled on. It didn't illuminate even a speck of dust as it made the shadows dance.

Lillian and I squeezed into the cramped closet, and she pulled the door closed behind us. Squaring her shoulders, she stared at the boards of the back wall with intent.

After uttering her magic-laced words in a breathy whisper, the wallboards rippled and revealed a purple door with a polished silver knob. Beyond the door was a hallway with four more doors leading to guest rooms.

I knew each room was decorated for one of the four physical elements. Needing a memory filled with happiness and laughter, I entered the first door on the left. The walls of the air room were sky blue, and little, fluffy clouds floated magically about the room. At the center, there was a high bed with a yellow blanket and pillow. Next to it was a side table with a pitcher of water and a glass along with the tools Lillian needed: a few crystals and a holder to catch the incense ashes.

As I removed my shoes, hat, and coat and climbed into the warm bed, Lillian pulled a stick of precious incense from a pouch at her waist. She lit it with a match, shook out the flame, and placed the stick in its holder. Standing at the head of the bed, she closed her eyes and inhaled deeply. Finally, she looked down at me.

"Have you chosen a memory, or would you like to just see what comes?"

"I have one in mind."

She nodded. "Be aware that the next time you fall asleep, you will relive a negative memory of equal proportion to this positive memory."

"I understand."

"Would you still like to continue?"

"Yes."

She nodded again. With the formalities over, we could finally get started. "Visualize the person you want to see or the place you want to go."

As her cool fingertips touched my temples, I closed my eyes. I thought about how that day had started as Lillian began to chant.

I'd almost made it out of the house in britches, but Aunt Vi had caught me before I could reach the door. I'd protested to Dad, but he just chuckled and reminded me Aunt Vi was here to ensure I was raised as a proper young lady.

Still, as I'd passed to go back upstairs to change, he'd slyly handed me a coin for the day ahead. As I squirmed in my periwinkle dress, Aunt Vi tried to brush my hair into some semblance of order.

Finally, she held up a mirror for me to see.

"You're such a beautiful girl, Anna," she encouraged.

It's not that I don't think I'm pretty or dislike being a girl, it's that I can't move properly in a dress.

But Aunt Vi had heard the protest before and had assured me I would learn.

"Thank you, Aunt Vi." I tried to smile sincerely.

"You're welcome, dear. Now, you be careful today."

"I will."

After swiftly kissing Aunt Vi and Dad, I ran from the house. Cy and Jack were already waiting for me on the stoop.

"What took you so long, Caill? We're going to be late," Cy complained. After noticing my dress, he rolled his eyes. "Oh, you had to put on your girl clothes."

I looked down at my dress self-consciously.

"You look pretty, Anna," Jack complemented as if Cy had never spoken. He reached out and touched the periwinkle ribbon at the end of my braid. "I like your ribbon."

I smiled at him, relieved. "Thank you, Jack."

"Enough with this girly stuff. Let's go," Cy pushed Jack onward and hurried ahead. I was glad I had to run to catch up because the movement helped me control my excitement. We had all been saving our allowances for months in preparation of this day.

When we finally turned the corner and beheld the colorful tents and flashing lights of the circus, we stopped in awe. My head spun, overwhelmed by what I saw. Two rows of tents lined the blocked-off street, leading to one giant, yellow big top. People crowded the avenues, consuming the festive atmosphere. One circus witch near us had fireballs orbiting his head like planets.

We stared at him with our jaws hanging open. Of course we'd seen magic before, but never had it been so blatant. Most witches used their magic quietly, and none of us had ever been to a healer.

The fire wielder noticed our attention and approached with a smile. Crouching down in front of us, he grabbed a pouch from his belt. From it, he poured a measure of sand into his palm. He whispered to the sand tenderly and stoked it with his fingertips. After a flash of fire, a delicate glass rose sat where the sand had been. We gasped then clapped to show our appreciation.

The fire witch smiled and held out the flower to me. "It's always polite to bring a lady flowers. Remember that, boys," he instructed, winking at Cy and Jack.

I cradled the still-warm gift in my hands. "Thank you." I beamed at him.

He raised his hand and nodded as though he were tipping an invisible hat.

Cy, Jack, and I marveled at the little piece of magic as the witch moved on to delight someone else.

"That's wonderful, Anna. Make sure you keep it safe," Jack advised, stroking the flower with his fingertip.

"I wish I could do that." Cy stared after the witch.

"Wishing for it isn't going to give you a witch's soul," Jack informed.

"I know that," Cy spat.

"Then why bother wishing?" Jack asked curiously.

"Twenty-three skidoo! Look at that." I pointed to a flock of witches circling the big top on brooms. Each broom had colored ribbons tied into the bristles so they fluttered behind like comet tails.

We rushed toward the big top to see the performances. The raised benches that held the audience were already crowded with people. We squeezed into the top corner, our arms pressed together in order to fit.

The electric lights were clouded by incense smoke as it hung in the room like fog.

Finally, the ringleader stepped into the performance area. He wore a yellow tuxedo with tails and a tall, black top hat.

"Ladies and gentleman," he called to the audience, and the crowd quieted. "Welcome to Broomhilt's Magical Mystical Circus!"

Everyone cheered with enthusiasm but stopped when the ringleader held up his hands.

"Our first performers, here to shock and amaze you, are Ed and Tess Spark!"

The man and woman who entered to applause wore matching black and blue outfits.

Tess Spark held a bunch of wire rings. She moved several yards away from Ed then faced him. The crowd hushed, waiting to see what they would do. A low rumbling sound filled the tent as if a thunderstorm were approaching. After pausing for effect, she threw a ring into the air.

Ed pointed at the ring, holding his forefinger and thumb like a gun. Pressing the hammer that was his thumb, a bolt of lightning shot out of his finger with a crack. It went right through the soaring ring, creating a wheel of electricity with spokes of crackling bolts.

The audience gasped and cheered as Ed continued to hit the targets, which Tess threw farther and faster.

While we were all awed, Jack seemed almost entranced by the performance. His mouth hung open, and he barely blinked. He was the loudest among the crowd as we cheered when Ed and Tess Spark took their bows.

"Our next performers are the Nereid Twins!" announced the sunflower of a ringleader.

Suddenly, the bright lights went out, and orbs of soft blue light appeared around the room. The audience was too amazed to clap as two blondes entered. One wore a long, flowing gown of seaweed green, and the other wore a bathing suit of the same color.

The one in the dress planted herself in the middle of the ring as the other began to climb a tall ladder leading to a short platform. As she climbed, her sister prepared the stage by conjuring a series of giant water bubbles, which she released to float about the room.

The audience held its breath as the climbing twin reached the platform. She stepped up to the edge, her bare toes hanging off the ledge, and raised her arms dramatically. With a controlled leap, she dove into the nearest bubble. Arching upward and kicking to gather speed, she jumped out of that bubble and soared through the air into another.

The floating water bubbles drifted about the hushed room, the water sparkling and shimmering in the blue light of the orbs. The diver gracefully executed an elaborate dance of swimming and sailing through the air as her sister maintained the water bubbles.

Eventually, the swimmer made her way to a lower bubble and exited, landing elegantly next to her sister. The crowd erupted as if they had no choice but to relieve the pressure of holding in the cheers.

"You've all heard stories about the magical creatures of myth and legend," the ringleader spun into the still dim tent. "Of brave heroes slaying beasts and saving maidens. In order to survive being hunted, magical creatures make pacts with witches. In exchange for being a familiar, a witch promises to protect a creature's identity from humans by shrouding its appearance in the humans' eyes.

Today, some of our familiars have agreed to show you their true forms."

As the electric lights came back on, three witches and their ordinary looking familiars joined the ringleader. There was a dog, a horse, and a snake.

"Behold!" the ringleader called as he pointed at the dog. With a wave from the dog's witch, the dog's appearance shimmered and revealed it had three heads. "The hellhound!" the ringleader announced to the gasping crowd. The hellhound wagged its tail and licked its witch's hands and face as she knelt down to pet it. The crowd clapped when it showed signs of friendliness.

Pointing at the horse, its appearance shimmered and it stretched out its glorious feathered wings. "The pegasus!" The audience ooed and ahed at the gorgeous winged horse.

Standing beside the last witch with the snake, the ringleader paused. We leaned forward in anticipation. The witch waved his hand at the snake, and its appearance shimmered. A blink later, the snake's head had widened to accommodate huge eyes, ears, and horns. Its long body had four legs ending in claws.

"The dragon!"

The dragon held its head proudly as it received its tribute of applause.

After the show was over, we left the big top, grateful for the fresh air.

A nearby stall sold refreshments in various colors. I hadn't realized how thirsty I was until I'd gulped down my blue drink.

I heard Jack snort into his white drink as if choking.

"Are you all right?" I asked, patting him on the back as he stared at me in shock.

Cy pointed at me and laughed.

"What?" I asked him, but he was laughing too hard to answer.

"Y-y-your hair," Jack stuttered.

I grabbed at the end of my braid and pulled my hair over my shoulder so I could see it. It was bright blue.

"What happened?" I moaned, panicking as I thought of Aunt Vi's reaction.

"Don't fret," the stall owner told us. "It'll wear off in a few hours."

I sighed in relief and looked at my friends. "Why hasn't your hair changed colors?"

They shrugged and downed the rest of their drinks. As I watched, their appearances changed, too. Cy grew a pair of antlers, and Jack sprouted wolf ears from the top of his head.

I laughed at their additions, glad only my hair had changed.

"What does it look like?" Cy demanded.

"You have deer antlers on your head," I laughed.

He reached up and touched his antlers then grinned.

"What about me?" Jack asked.

Cy laughed at Jack's ears. They looked so fuzzy and soft. I reached over and stroked them. "Can you feel that, Jack?"

His face reddened. "Um, yes."

"You have animal ears on your head," Cy burst.

I kept petting Jack's new ears, and he clenched his eyes shut as if he were embarrassed.

"I think they're adorable," I announced.

That sent Cy into another fit of laughter. Jack grabbed my wrist to still my hand. He gently let go and stepped out of reach, avoiding my eyes.

Taken aback by Jack's reaction and disappointed I

couldn't stroke his soft ears, I looked around for something else to do.

"Do you want to play games?" I asked, successfully distracting them.

The first game we tried was a test of strength. Players were to hit a pedal with a hammer, and a board measured their strength. Cy stepped up to go first.

"Watch this." He grinned as his lifted the hammer.

Smashing it down on the pedal, a ball at the bottom of the board traveled to the top and burst into a firework of magic dust.

I clapped, and Cy handed Jack the hammer.

"Too easy," Cy boasted.

Jack also sent the ball into a burst of color.

When I held out my hand to Jack for the hammer, he cautioned, "Be careful. It's heavy."

"She can do it," Cy chided Jack for babying me.

"I know she can," Jack snapped.

I swung the hammer, and the ball exploded.

"Good job," Jack congratulated.

"I knew you could do it." Cy smiled.

We each earned a piece of candy as a prize.

Next, Jack wanted to try a shooting game. Each player was given a rifle with ten pellets. The goal was to hit eight of ten floating targets. Jack only hit seven, but we cheered for him anyway.

Cy wanted to try a game that tested magical ability, but for humans, it was just a guessing game. There were five different cards in a set of fifteen. The goal was to guess five of ten correctly before flipping them over.

Cy was so disappointed when he lost that I told him I'd win him the prize, which was a magic crystal. It was pretty but completely useless to humans.

I barely won; my last chance happened to be a good

guess. The crystal shard was a murky white, like frozen lake water. I dropped it into Cy's cupped hands.

"Thanks, Caill. You're the best," he praised, clapping me on the shoulder.

I smiled, pleased at the admiration and the joy I'd given him.

I knew it was time to leave soon. Dad and Aunt Vi were expecting me for dinner, but I couldn't go home with blue hair.

I reached for my braid and realized my hair had come undone. The wavy locks flew free, and my ribbon was gone. More importantly, my bright blue hair had muted a little and seemed to be darkening to its normal chestnut color.

Just a little longer.

I scanned the nearby tents to see if there was anything that could occupy us for the time we had left. A dark blue tent with silver stars beckoned to me.

"What's in there?" I asked my friends.

"I don't know. Let's find out," Cy responded, pocketing the crystal I'd given him.

We pushed aside the sheer curtain, which acted as a door. Before we could step inside, an airy voice called, "One at a time."

"It's a fortune teller," Jack whispered, pointing at the sign on the back wall of the entrance.

"I'll go first," I volunteered, intrigued by the prospect of a new experience.

The boys nodded and stepped back. I entered the dim, smoky tent. A single candle lit the small, round table and the woman behind it. She had beautiful dark skin with black eyes that reflected the candle's flame. Her shadowy, curly hair was wild and free. On the shelves behind her, there was an assortment of crystals, stones, cards, pouches, bowls, and a teapot with cups.

"Please, have a seat." She motioned to the chair across from her. I did as instructed and waited.

"What would you like to know?" she asked.

I shrugged. "Whatever is important, I guess."

She nodded with a slight smile and pulled a bowl and a drawstring pouch from the shelf behind her. Holding the pouch out to me, she told me to grab a handful of herbs.

I did as she bid and seized some of the long, dried herbs, being careful not to crush them.

After taking the stems from me, she held the ends to the candle and blew them out once they'd caught fire. Then, she put the smoldering herbs into the bowl and stared intently at the rising smoke.

Her black eyes soon lost focus as if she were no longer present.

"You will reconnect with your soulmate in this life. In fact, he's already near and dear to you." She smiled at the prospect of my great love.

Cy's and Jack's smiling faces flashed in my mind. I'd never really thought much about love before. Still, my heart skipped a beat, and I leaned in with interest.

"He sees you as an equal and will cherish you above all things."

They both see me as an equal. "How can I tell who he is?"

She frowned a little and seemed to be asking the smoke my question.

I held my breath.

"I see he already treasures something of yours."

...*The crystal...Cy is my soulmate.*

FIVE

The warm glow I'd gotten when I'd realized Cy was my soulmate stayed with me even as I woke from the Living Memory. I remembered how everything had changed after that revelation.

I let myself bask in contentment. Even though my mind knew Cy was dead, my body felt as if I'd just seen him. It wouldn't be until I awoke from my next sleep that I would feel his loss again, and I had an eternity until the next morning.

I took the glass of water Lillian held out to me and thanked her.

Refreshed, I hopped out of bed. The floor felt cold on my feet even through my stockings. After padding over to my bag, I pulled out the dough and paid Lillian for her services.

"Since I'm working an active case, I'll probably see you again tomorrow," I told her.

She nodded solemnly and fixed the blankets while I put on my shoes, hat, and coat.

Lillian escorted me to her sitting room. A man in a smart gray suit stood when we entered.

"Good morning, Jim," Lillian greeted. "I'll be right with you."

She accompanied me downstairs to Starlight Avenue. "Where would you like to come out?" she asked.

"The public exit nearest to Madison and Oak."

She created my personal guide and let it fly. I followed it obediently through the tunnels until I reached an iron gate guarded by a short yet intimidating man. He reached up and snuffed out my guide as it stopped by his doorway.

"Goin' out?" he asked.

"Yeah."

He nodded and opened the gate for me. I climbed the stairs into a mausoleum, where I left through another iron gate. The cemetery was cold and quiet, even for a cemetery. I walked the brick paths as if I belonged there.

After exiting the stone arch on Oak, I turned north toward Madison. I buried myself deep in my coat as the winter wind burned my face.

The address Jesse had given me turned out to be a brownstone, squished between its neighbors like a moon pie. Though I was twenty minutes early, Jesse waited for me on the stoop, hunched into himself as if he'd been fighting the cold for a while.

He stood when he recognized me. His eyes found mine, and I halted my approach. It was as though my brain had shut down, and I couldn't look at him and do anything else at the same time.

He closed the remaining distance between us, and with every step, my pulse quickened.

Was he this tall this morning?

I felt a little lightheaded before I remembered how to

breathe. Prying my gaze from his, I looked at the blue door of Leo's house.

"You're early," I stalled to get my thoughts in order. "I'm sorry if you waited long. Any sign that Mr. Nimzic returned?"

"No," he answered in his rich baritone, his cool demeanor still intact.

"Do you happen to have a key?" I still didn't make eye contact but stared at his coat lapel.

"No, I don't."

"Is there any way to magic us in?"

When he didn't answer, I took a chance and looked up at his face. He sucked his plump lower lip in thought as if contemplating the mysteries of the universe. As he released his newly-moistened lip, I shoved my hands deep into my coat pockets to stop myself from reaching for the soft, pink skin.

"I wish I could help, but Leo has a magical seal, which protects his home and those inside from outside magic."

After pulling a small leather case from my coat pocket, I held it up. "Lockpick it is then."

He rewarded me with an impressed smile, which knocked the wind out of me. "You're a clever one."

I didn't trust myself to respond, so I hid my enflamed face and hiked to the door. The lock was simple enough to pick. We entered quietly and closed it behind us.

Leo's home wasn't what I'd imagined a high priest's house would be. It was ordinary with average furniture and tasteful wallpaper. The lights were off, but overcast light filtered through the many windows.

We started on the ground floor. The sitting room was warm and welcoming with a fireplace and fresh flowers in a vase on the coffee table. They must've been put out fairly recently because they weren't wilted and there was still water in the crystal vase. Not even a book was out of place. The dining room table was dusted and polished and was decorated with barely-burned candlesticks. The kitchen was clean, with not so much as a dirty cup marring its immaculate presentation. Herbs grew cheerfully in pots on the windowsill as if loved and well cared for.

"Is it normally this clean?" I asked Jesse as we moved toward the stairs to the second floor.

"Yes, Leo is meticulous."

At the top of the landing, there was an elaborate geometric mural painted on the wall; each overlapping shape was a different color. I stopped to examine it. Its elegant strokes and melding of shapes were breathtaking. Just as I was turning away, a tiny imperfection caught my attention. In the corner, a hair's width of paint had been scratched.

"What's that?"

Jesse moved in close to me and squinted at the blemish. His proximity made my head spin. I'd thought he'd only affected me so much that morning because I was hollowed out following the after effects of Living Memory. But I was much more aware of him in the afterglow of seeing Cy, when the craving wasn't distracting me.

I stepped away from him, guilt chewing on my carnal thoughts.

"I can't believe you noticed such a small nick. I didn't even see it. Leo's seal is broken."

I would've felt flattered had his statement not had such serious implications. "That means someone could've used magic to enter his house or put a spell on him?" I asked for clarification.

"Yes," Jesse confirmed, his brow knitting in concern.

"Let's keep going," I instructed.

At the top of the stairs, Jesse pointed to the door on the

right. "That's Leo's altar room where he does all his magic. We can't go in there."

"Is it sealed? What about my lockpick?"

He shook his head. "This one is different. Serious harm will come to anyone who tries to enter without Leo present, unless he works them into the seal's spell-work."

I nodded, and we went to the door on the left, to what Jesse said was Leo's bedroom. Unlike the ground floor, Leo's bedroom was not the perfect example of order. While his bed was made, his closet and dresser drawers were all opened. Clothes spilled onto the floor, but nothing seemed broken.

A frame on his nightstand had been put face down as if someone couldn't stand to be looked at by the person in the photograph. I set it upright, and a sultry woman stared back at me. She had flapper-short, blonde hair and dark eyes. The corner of the photograph read: "To Leo, my sun. You drive me wild, your Rose." There was also a bright red lip print next to the signature.

"Do you know Rose?" I asked Jesse, holding up the photograph.

He nodded. "Yes, Rose is a performer at The Black Moon. She and Leo have been seeing each other for a while."

"Maybe he's with her," I suggested.

He shook his head. "She was performing last night at The Black Moon when Leo was supposed to meet me there."

I put the photograph back on the nightstand and continued to look around. His closet and dresser were missing a lot of clothes. A quick peek into his attached bathroom showed that his toiletries were gone as well.

"Do you know where he keeps his suitcase?"

"Under his bed, I think."

I dropped down on my knees and peeked under the bed. There was no suitcase in sight, but there was a slit cut into the seam of the mattress. A red satin cord peeked through the hole. Pulling on it, a red drawstring bag fell out. I picked it up and stood.

"What's this?" I turned to Jesse, showing him the bag.

He squinted in bewilderment. "It looks like a charm bag. Where did you find it?"

"It was tucked into a hole in the mattress. What's it a charm for?"

"I don't know. What's inside?"

I opened the pouch, and we both peered into it. There were two small bundles of hair, one blond and one black. There was also a pin and a measure of black powder.

"What kind of charm is it?" I looked up into Jesse's unreadable face.

He met my eyes, and I suddenly realized how close we were standing.

"Looks like a charm for driving away nightmares," he answered. "But there are some unusual components. May I borrow it? Perhaps some ingredients can tell us where Leo has been of late."

I paused, thinking I shouldn't let potential evidence out of my possession. *Can I trust him?*

Jesse's cool demeanor gave nothing away. He was like a puzzle begging to be solved. I couldn't deny I was intrigued. He'd sucked me into his labyrinth before I'd realized it.

Give a little. Get a little. Besides, there doesn't appear to be a case here. I smiled warmly at Jesse and handed him the charm bag. "Did Mr. Nimzic tell you that he'd been having nightmares?"

"No."

"Perhaps that was one of the reasons he was acting strange?"

Jesse pursed his lips in thought.

I met his eyes again, unsure of how he would take what I was going to say next. *Is this goodbye?* "Mr. Hunt, in light of the current evidence, it appears your friend left of his own accord. He certainly left in a hurry, but there are no signs of a struggle. Even the door was locked. I'll admit that it's strange his seal was broken, but it's also possible that was an accident."

"But that doesn't make any sense. It's so unlike him to leave without telling anyone," he said to himself.

His lost expression pulled at my heart. I reached out and put my hand on his arm. He jumped and met my eyes with a surprised and unsure expression.

"I'm sorry you're worried, but it's good news. Right? It means he's fine. He just isn't here. My advice is to leave him a note and wait for him to return. Is there anything else I can do to help?"

I thought his eyes softened a bit before he closed his expression again.

"Ms. Caill, can I still hire you to find him? Even if he isn't missing, he's still somewhere. I'll rest easier if I know where he is."

I nodded. "Of course, but he'll probably return on his own soon."

"Thank you."

SIX

FJOLNIR

I stood in the kitchen, looking out the window at the overcast day. Squinting at the clouds, I willed them to hold the snow until after the full moon.

I managed not to squirm as Raven wrapped his arms around my stomach from behind. He rested his cheek on my shoulder for a moment. Then, I felt his breath hot in my ear.

"Good morning," he whispered, nibbling my earlobe.

As his hands started to drift down to the waistband of my pants, I stepped out of his embrace.

"His dose is probably wearing off. I should give him another," I declared by way of excuse.

Raven's dark eyes glinted with jealousy. I gritted my teeth into a smile and reached up to stroke his cheek.

"Don't be like that. You know I'd rather it was you, but I don't want to hurt you. After him, this'll all be over, and we'll be equals."

He leaned into my hand and sighed.

I moved in slowly until our lips were barely an inch apart. I could feel his desire as he quivered, and heat waves rolled off him in pulses.

"I'm feeling a little low on energy if you'd like to give me a boost when I'm finished."

He panted with anticipation, and I took that as a yes. I covered his mouth with mine as he moaned and melted into compliance.

"Meet me in the barn. This'll only take a second," I promised.

After going to our bedroom, I opened the little tin we'd purchased from Arthur the week prior. After dabbing it on my fingers, I spread the balm on my lips, being careful not to lick them.

Before I entered the bedroom adjacent to ours, I conjured my most charming smile. At the sound of the door, Leo stirred from his drugged sleep. I sauntered over to where he was tied to the bed.

"Good morning, Sleepy."

He cracked his groggy, confused eyes.

"Fjolnir?" he croaked.

He blinked a few times, and I could tell the spell was starting to wear thin like fog dissipating in the morning sun.

Sitting on the bed next to him, I leaned over and kissed his mouth. As I pulled away, he licked his lips. Seconds later, his eyes clouded with infatuation and desire, and he pulled at his bonds to get to me.

His fervent eyes followed me as I went to the dresser and poured him a cup of tea.

"You must be thirsty. Would you like something to drink? I bet you have a headache. This will help."

He lifted his head and drank deeply when I held the cup to his lips.

"Good boy," I encouraged, stroking his hair.

After putting the teacup back, I watched as his eyes drooped with forced sleep.

"Don't worry, Leo. Just sleep. I promise your dreams will all be pleasant and of me."

He smiled drunkenly and fell asleep.

That should keep him out for a few hours. Now, to deal with Raven.

The bracing cold helped me prepare for what I needed to do as I breathed deep and opened the barn door.

Raven was ready for me, lying on the altar with his shirt unbuttoned.

"What took you so long?" he complained, standing as I approached him.

I smiled seductively. "I'm worth the wait."

He dropped to his knees and unbuttoned my pants. "I know you are."

SEVEN

ANNA

Even though I'd agreed to try to find Leo, Jesse still took my advice and left him a note.

After we'd relocked the door, Jesse gave me his calling card so I could contact him about the case.

"I'll call you tomorrow," I promised.

"I'd like to accompany you in your investigation."

While the idea of spending more time with Jesse made me tingle, I knew there were some things in this business that were easier to do alone.

"I'll be more effective alone at this point in the investigation. I'm sure you'll be a lot of help later. Please wait for my call."

He nodded his understanding. "Call me if you need anything at all."

"I will," I assured him.

We parted ways. As he turned the corner of Madison and Union, I knocked at one of Leo's neighbor's door. It didn't take long before a smiling, middle-aged woman answered.

"Yes?" she asked, wiping flour-dusted hands on her apron.

"I'm sorry to bother you, ma'am, but may I ask you about your neighbor, Leo?"

She blushed scarlet, and her eyes widened.

"Please, come in." She stepped aside for me to enter.

I followed her through her clean, but well lived-in, house to her kitchen. She'd been making holiday cookies. Her countertops were covered in flour and dough that had been rolled and was waiting to be cut.

"Would you like some tea?"

"Thank you, ma'am. That would be most welcome."

She motioned for me to have a seat at her kitchen table as she put a kettle on to boil and collected the sugar, milk, and cups.

I waited patiently as it was clear she was gathering her thoughts while she prepared the refreshments. After a while, she sat down across from me and poured me a cup of tea. I stirred in two lumps of sugar and a dash of milk. After sipping at the warm liquid, I smiled.

"Thank you, ma'am."

She nodded and pointed at a plate of freshly-frosted cookies. "Feel free to have a cookie as well."

"Thank you." I nibbled at the end of a yellow frosted star and smiled to put her at ease. "Ma'am, I'm looking for your neighbor, Leo Nimzic. Do you know where he is?"

She looked down into her cup as her face reddened again. "I'm not one to gossip or judge," she started then stalled as though she didn't know how to continue.

"When did you see him last?" I asked gently, hoping simple, direct questions would encourage her to spill.

"Last night," she admitted.

"What time?"

"Around eight."

"Did you see him leave his house?"

"I heard an automobile door slam, so I looked outside."

"Leo was getting into a motorcar? Was he alone, or was he with someone?" *If her face gets any redder, she might faint.*

"He was with a man."

"Did you recognize the man?"

"I've seen him a few times recently, but I didn't know they were…"

"What did the man look like?"

"I never got a good look, but his hair is blond."

"What happened?" I reached out and covered her hand with mine. She looked up and met my eyes. "It's all right. You can tell me. What did you see?"

"They were…kissing," she whispered.

My mind skidded to a halt. *That was…unexpected.*

Leo's neighbor grew more flustered with the passing of each silent moment.

"All right, what happened then?"

"I don't know. I was so shocked I closed the curtain. It sounded like they drove away."

"Thank you for telling me, ma'am."

"I'm sorry if you're a friend of his. I didn't mean to surprise you."

"It's fine. You've been a great help." I smiled at her reassuringly and finished my cookie and tea.

Thanking her again, I hailed a dimbox when I got to the main street. It was a fifteen-minute ride to my house, but my mind raced all the way there.

Leo is a homosexual? Then, what about Rose? Is that why her photograph was face down? If he was worried about how Jesse would take it, that could be why he has been acting uncharacteristically of late. It's understandable why he wouldn't tell anyone he was going off with his lover. Who is this guy with the blond hair? Is he a witch, too? Is he a human? Where did they meet? If I can figure that out, I may be able to find Leo.

I paid the cabbie when he dropped me off at my front door. Taking a few deep breaths, I prepared myself to go inside. I locked away all my worries, which was significantly easier while riding the high of Living Memory. Placing a calm smile on my face, I entered my home.

I removed my hat and coat and put them on the hooks near the door. It didn't take Aunt Vi long to leave her needlepoint in the sitting room and come to greet me. Her stern expression softened only a little as I kissed her on her wrinkled cheek.

"Good afternoon, Aunt Vi. How are you?"

"I'd be a lot better if you'd have come home last night," she scolded.

"As you can see, I'm ducky."

"Nice young ladies shouldn't stay out all night," she instructed as if for the first time.

"Maybe I'm not nice," I countered playfully.

She sputtered on cue. "Anna!"

I smiled sweetly. "Where's Dad?"

"You know very well he's in his study," she harrumphed.

"Thanks, Aunt Vi. Love you," I called over my shoulder as I ankled down the hall to Dad's study.

I opened the sliding wooden doors and entered the study. It didn't matter how much Aunt Vi cleaned; there was always dust from the books. *I wish Dad would sit somewhere else.*

"Is that my girl finally come home?" Dad asked hoarsely from his winged armchair by the fireside.

"The one and only." I smiled, kissing him on the forehead and trying to ignore the ever-growing infestation of gray in his hair.

Sitting in a nearby armchair, I watched him put down his book and pick up a pipe.

"Where did you get that?" I demanded, pointing at the offending object.

He looked down at the pipe, surprised as though it had just materialized without cause. "I've no idea."

"Hand it over." I stood and held out my hand.

"But Anna…" he practically whined.

"I don't want to hear it. You know what the healers say."

He reluctantly handed me the pipe. "The doctors don't agree."

"The doctors can argue all they want, but the witches have long known the toxins from smoking cause these problems."

He grumbled under his breath.

Sitting back down, I clutched the pipe like it was stealing my father from me.

Dad leaned forward in his chair, resting his elbows on his knees. "Tell me, my girl, are you working any interesting cases?"

I smiled at his curiosity and need for adventure. "I was hired on a missing person's case this morning."

"Oh? What is it? Kidnapping? Murder?"

I laughed. "I don't think so. It looks like the fella just left for a secret rendezvous."

"Ah. Who hired you? A jealous wife? A jilted girlfriend?"

"No, just a friend. As far as I know." *Now that I think about it, who's to say Jesse isn't a jilted lover?*

That thought made me a little grummy.

"Well, you just let me know if you need any of my expertise."

"I thought you'd taught me everything you knew."

"I've still got a couple of tricks up my sleeve." He winked at me.

I laughed. "I know who to ask if I get stuck."

Standing, I said, "I have to get ready to see Jack. I'll ask him to pick me up here so you can see him, too."

After handing the pipe over to Aunt Vi for destruction, I rang Jack at work.

"Jack O'Keefe, *The Times*," Jack answered his desk phone.

"What's a girl got to do to get a little attention from you, Jack O'Keefe?"

"Anna? It's been a while. How've you been?"

"Yeah, what's with the cold shoulder, Jack? I haven't heard from you in weeks."

"Oh, just busy with work," he hedged.

Liar. "Well, listen: wherever you want to go tonight is on me."

"I don't know, Anna. I'm drowning in copy."

"Don't you dare, Jack O'Keefe. I don't care how busy you are. You have to celebrate your birthday with me."

"All right," he laughed. "I'll pick you up at six."

"That's just fine, but pick me up at home. You better come armed with an apology, too. Dad's upset he hasn't heard from you."

"Thanks for the warning. See you later."

"Jack, wait." I stopped him from hanging up.

"What is it?"

"Happy birthday, Jack."

"Thanks, Anna."

EIGHT

I rang Maggie next. She answered cheerfully. "Anna Caill, private detective's office. How may I help you?"

"Maggie, it's Anna."

"Anna! What's cookin'? I saw your note about a missing person's case this morning. What can I do to help?"

I smiled at her upbeat eagerness. "Do I have any messages?"

"No messages. But Mrs. Ransen stopped by to pay her bill. Her missing ring was pawned by her son to pay gambling debts, just like you said. She thanked you for looking into it and promised to refer clients your way."

"Swell. About the missing person's case, I need you to look into something for me. There's a club called The Black Moon. Find out when a performer named Rose will be there next."

"I've heard of that place. It's not easy for humans to get into alone."

"I'll find a way in. Just get me the time Rose will be there."

"Ab-so-lute-ly."

"Thanks, Maggie."

After hanging up, I climbed the stairs to my room to doll up for my best friend's birthday.

As always, my bedroom felt like a safe haven where I could relax and be myself. I didn't have to keep up the pretense of being happy.

I took off my shoes and flopped face down on my bed.

Why has Jack been avoiding me? Did my façade slip? Maybe it's not me at all. Maybe he finally found a woman.

I thought of all the women who'd chased Jack while he was just a college student in Oxford bags. He never seemed to notice them, at least not while he was around me.

I could never understand how he was alone. He was my favorite person, always kind and caring. He deserved all the happiness life had to give.

Though I suppose it's only natural that when he finds someone, he'll have less time for me. My chest felt tight like my lungs weren't working. I crossed my arms over my head and turned my face toward my nightstand, resting my forehead on my forearm and taking a deep breath of fresh air. I stared at my treasures, thinking of better days. Beside a photograph of Mom and Dad as young newlyweds, there was a delicate glass rose and a tarot card.

Why does he smile? Hanging upside down by your foot would be painful at most, uncomfortable at best.

I knew I didn't have time to brood. I had to be the picture of fun when Jack arrived. I had to ensure he had no doubt in his mind that I was happy. Jack was the reason I pretended. It would hurt him too much to see me in pain, and I never wanted to hurt Jack.

I remembered the months following Cy's death. It was natural for us both to mourn him, but Jack's awareness of my sorrow seemed to double his own. He'd managed to support me, but I hated that pained look in his eyes whenever he handled me gently as if I'd break. I didn't mind my own pain. While I was prepared to wallow for the rest of my life, I didn't want to bring Jack with me. It was for him that I went to that medium and later used Living Memory to achieve functionality.

I spent the next couple hours dressing, applying cosmetics, and arranging my hair. When six rolled around, I was ready.

Jack was on time as always. I opened the door when he knocked.

He looked airtight in his charcoal pinstriped suit. The color made his aquamarine eyes seem bright and welcoming. He removed his hat as he entered.

"Hello, Gorgeous." He smiled at me.

"Hello, Stranger." I gave him my best smile then went in for a hug.

The moment I felt his gentle embrace, I was at ease. The ever-lurking darkness was still there, but Jack's light kept it at bay for the time being. It was those moments that told me that if I pretended long enough, I could convince myself I was all right.

"Happy birthday, Jack. I missed you."

His answering smile was a gift. "Maybe I should be busy more often," he suggested.

"Don't you dare."

He chuckled.

Dad was overjoyed when Jack and I entered his study. "Jackie Boy, how have you been? Happy birthday." He stood to embrace Jack.

"Thank you, Sir. I'm sorry I haven't been by for a visit."

Dad waved his hand dismissively as if he hadn't sulked when he didn't see Jack. "Work is work. Besides, you're a big-time newspaperman now. I read your article on Lucky Lindy earlier this year. It was very well done."

"Thank you, Sir."

They talked for a while about Jack's job and what Charles Lindbergh was like in person. As the conversation seemed to be coming to an end, Dad turned to me.

"Anna, my girl, go ask your Aunt Vi about dinner. Will you?"

I squinched my face, knowing he was trying to get me out of the room for some reason. I did as I was asked, but when I returned, the study doors were closed to me. After a few minutes, Jack exited, looking somber.

"What was that about?" I asked Jack as we headed down the hall to put on our coats.

He tried for an unconcerned smile and failed. "Your father had a request."

"What was it?" My face darkened. "It wasn't for a pipe, was it?"

He laughed. "He did throw that one in at the end, yes."

"Well, what was it?"

"I'll let you know if I can honor it."

We slid into Jack's motorcar, and he was quiet and thoughtful as he drove.

I guess he's still thinking about whatever Dad wanted.

Finally, he broke the silence. "Do you remember that time we were invited to play baseball with the older neighborhood kids?"

"Sure." I nodded. "When they invited Cy to bring his two friends, they didn't realize I was a girl."

He looked at me sharply. "He was so angry when they said you couldn't play, telling them you were as good as any of them."

"I remember I was really surprised by their animosity."

I smiled over at him. "But it was what you said that gave me courage, Jack. Do you remember? You told me I didn't have to prove myself to them."

"He didn't agree."

"You fellas always took different approaches, but I still knew you both saw me as an equal."

Jack pulled up to a swanky uptown restaurant and handed the valet his keys. He must've called in a reservation because a table was waiting for us. The large, round room of the restaurant had white walls with gilded, framed nature paintings. Columns circled the round tables full of patrons. In the center, under a glass dome, a string quartet serenaded the guests.

After Jack ordered our food, an awkward silence settled between us. Just as I opened my mouth to ask what was wrong, Jack brought up work.

"So have you been working on any interesting cases?"

I frowned and shrugged. "I was hired on a missing person's case today." Leaning toward him, so no one could overhear, I continued. "Actually, I could really use some of your sources for a case I'm working."

"Oh yeah? What do you need?"

"Well, my client hired me to find his friend. Apparently, he's been acting strangely as of late, and he was supposed to meet my client but never showed. We went to his house, and there were no signs of a struggle. It looks like he just packed up and left. But get this: his neighbor said she saw him necking another man in a motorcar when he was supposed to be meeting my client. However, my client only mentioned a female lover."

His eyebrows rose slightly. "What do you need from me?"

"The guy who's missing is a high priest. I need information on him and where he might go to get away. Finding out who his lover is may prove to be valuable as well. Also, I'm starting to question my client's relationship with the missing person. Discovering more about him could help, too."

"Names?"

"The missing person is Leo Nimzic, and my client is Jesse Hunt." I sighed unintentionally when I thought of Jesse.

"I'll see what I can dig up."

"Thanks, Jack."

We talked about work for a while as we listened to the music. I asked after Jack's family, and he updated me on his nieces and nephews. He gradually started to loosen up. After we ate, we danced a little. All in all, it was shaping up to be a pleasant evening. I smiled easily, and Jack seemed to be enjoying his birthday.

When it was finally time to leave, we waited under the awning for the valet to bring the motorcar. I stepped in close to Jack, huddling in the winter air for warmth.

"What have you actually been doing these past few weeks?" I asked before I could stop myself from ruining our lovely time.

"I've been working."

"Come on, Jack. You've been in the newspaper game for a while now, and you've never worked this much," I pushed.

"I've also been thinking," he admitted.

"What's on your mind?"

He looked into my eyes seriously as if he could see my broken soul. I stilled, frozen by his solemn gaze. It'd been a long time since I'd seen that look on Jack.

His tone was measured and quiet. "Anna, we've known each other almost our entire lives. Why won't you open up to me? You don't have to pretend to be happy or that you aren't in pain. Won't you let me in? When you pretend like this, it makes me think you don't trust me or care about me anymore."

My heart sank. *Did I really think I was fooling Jack?* "You're wrong, Jack. It's because I care about you that I act this way. Why should you be in pain just because I am? The only reason I'm as functional as I am is that I have to pretend for you."

He reached out and grabbed my hand. "This isn't what I want for you. I want to help you heal."

"You are," I whispered, trying to soothe the pain in his voice.

"No, I'm not." He clenched his teeth. "You live in your own world, beyond my reach, tormented by shadows of the past. I know you use Living Memory, and I can guess what you relive," he said bitterly.

I wasn't even shocked Jack had figured it out. I looked away and didn't respond.

"You used it today, didn't you? I can tell by how casually you said his name. You never say his name aloud otherwise."

Jack has always been observant when it comes to how I'm feeling.

I used my eyes to plead with him. "Jack, please. This is how I need it to be. You're my sanctuary. I always feel safe and comfortable with you. Please don't take that away from me."

His expression was pained, but he pulled me into an embrace. "Fine, I'll be whatever you need me to be."

NINE

As always when I knew I'd have a nightmare, I went to my office to sleep. Streetlamps shone through the semicircle window, creating a sea of shadows. I didn't bother turning on the lights. I removed my hat and coat as I shuffled through my office. I hung them up and clicked on my desk lamp.

A note in Maggie's sprawling handwriting lay on the desk informing me that Rose would be at The Black Moon the following evening.

The glow from having seen Cy had practically worn off, and my limbs grew heavy in anticipation of sleep. I didn't have the motivation to wash my face or change for bed. I removed my shoes and stretched out on the couch, covering myself with a tan knit blanket Aunt Vi had made.

I welcomed the nightmarish memory. At least I didn't have to think about my conversation with Jack.

Almost everyone had lost someone in the war. But while I

wallowed in my own loss, everyone else seemed to drown the pain in the roaring gaiety of fast living.

Though I'd embraced the pain, I couldn't stand hurting Jack, Dad, or Aunt Vi anymore. Of course, they expected me to be depressed, but they were worried I'd never move on. I hadn't planned on it. I guess they knew me too well.

I'd thought my heart was so far beyond broken that nothing could be worse. Then, Jack looked at me with eyes of jagged sea glass, and I knew I had to do something.

It took a while, but I'd finally found Benji, a witch who trusted me enough to take me to Starlight Avenue. I'd convinced him that just because Dad was a PI, and I was his apprentice, that didn't mean I'd snitch to the coppers. I'm sure my sob story and haggard appearance helped just as much as the truth spell he'd cast on me.

Benji led me to Alice's tunnel door and introduced me to the medium before leaving us.

Alice had pale blonde hair and unfocused, light eyes. She waved for me to follow her in. The door from Starlight Avenue led into a candlelit basement. At the center of the room was a circular table covered in black satin. Shelves filled with unlabeled bottles, jars, and boxes leaned against the rough-hewn, stone walls, and a fat, iron stove glowed in the corner.

I sat at the table as Alice instructed. Taking the chair across, she addressed me in a quiet, blurry voice.

"You are here to contact a loved one who has passed beyond the veil?"

"Yes."

"What is the name?"

"Cyril Jenson."

"And when did he depart?"

"Six months ago."

"What was your relationship?"

"We were lovers and childhood friends."

She nodded and reached out for me to take her small, cold hands. She closed her pale eyes and called in an otherworldly, wispy voice.

"Mae, are you there?"

The candles around the room flickered but didn't go out.

Alice smiled slightly. "Hello, Mae. I hope you are well."

She paused as if listening to a response only she could hear.

"I am here with Anna Caill. She wants to contact her lost love, Cyril Jenson. Could you find him for us?"

She paused again then thanked the spirit.

With every silent moment that passed, my muscles tensed with anxiety, and I had to remind myself to breathe.

After a while, Alice frowned.

"How strange." She opened her eyes and focused on me with a sad expression. "I'm sorry, but your lover isn't there."

My brow furrowed in confusion. "I don't understand. What does that mean?"

"The only explanation I have is that his spirit has moved on to his next life."

"Why did you say it was strange?"

"Spirits don't usually move on that quickly..." She hesitated. "It means he had nothing to hold onto in this life...and that he wasn't waiting for someone else to join him."

Though she spoke gently, her words still kicked me in the gut.

"But the fortune teller said we were soulmates. Why wouldn't he wait for me?"

She shook her head. "I have no gift for divination.

However, if you are soulmates, you will see him in the next life. He may not be your lover, but perhaps a family member or friend. Unless…"

"Unless what?"

"Unless you did something he found unforgivable. If that were the case, he could want to avoid you for a lifetime or two. He could even have broken the bond that links your souls."

An ominous feeling overcame me, and my mind raced to figure out what I could've done. "You aren't even worth it," I heard Cy spit in my mind. *He died believing I preferred Jack to him. He would've seen that as an unforgivable betrayal. But it isn't true!*

My mind went blank, and a dissenting voice snuck in. *But why are you here? You came to say goodbye to Cy, hoping to talk to him one more time and let him go. That was for Jack. Wasn't it? Aren't you just choosing Jack over Cy?*

What? No.

Cy was heartbroken when he thought you'd be with Jack if he died. And look, all you can do is think about how you're hurting Jack and how to make it better.

But I'm not with Jack. We're the same friends we've always been.

Cy didn't think so. He wouldn't want you to be friends with Jack anymore.

I pictured Jack's reaction if I told him we couldn't be friends because that's what Cy would've wanted.

That's ridiculous. Cy was wrong. If we could've only talked about it, he would've seen that. We've all been friends forever. He would've remembered that and seen the truth.

"I need to talk to him," I pleaded with Alice.

Alice bit her lip in hesitation.

"Please," I begged, a sob catching in my throat.

She sighed and shook her head. "There is a way, but it

will not be real. You can relive memories of the past, though there are side effects, and that path is dangerous. Most who traverse it never fully live in the present again."

Relive memories? I can see Cy again? If I do that, then I'll have no problem acting normal for Jack, Dad, and Aunt Vi.

I reached toward her suggestion desperately. "How? What do I need to do?"

She grimaced but continued. "The spell is called Living Memory. I know a witch who can perform it."

"Please, how do I find this witch?"

She still looked reluctant. "I can arrange an introduction." Her distant, pale eyes became fierce as a sharpened blade glinting in the moonlight. They demanded my attention. "I advise you not to undergo such a venture in your current state. Wait until some time has passed and the natural grieving process has given you space. This spell is addictive. You could waste the rest of your life chasing the past."

"That's fine," I said soberly.

TEN

I felt only a little morbid when I awoke. The realization that Cy may have broken our link and abandoned our soulmate bond was on my mind daily, so reliving it didn't hurt too badly. It was early but not indecently so. I went to the bathroom and removed my cosmetics from the night before.

My urge to go to Lillian wasn't intolerable. Still, I had work to do and thought it best to see her before I continued my investigation.

I went to the little diner near my office and ordered a greasy breakfast and a pot of coffee. I was musing in a corner booth, dipping burnt toast into practically raw eggs when a familiar witch slid into the seat across from me.

"Hey there, lady detective." Benji smiled as I twitched at his adjective.

"Hey, man wi—"

He stopped me with a look, and I smiled innocently.

"You haven't called me in a while," he pointed out, snatching a cold, diced potato from my plate and popping it into his mouth. "Don't you love me anymore?"

I rolled my eyes at him. "I haven't needed your services of late."

He looked amused. "That can't be right. I'm all kinds of useful."

"You know, for someone who was worried about me being a snitch, you don't seem to have any qualms about doing it yourself."

He shrugged. "I prefer the term informant, and I have principles. I'm not going to give up the goods on someone just for being born that way, but hurting others isn't copacetic."

His hand snaked toward my plate again, and I pushed it at him. He helped himself, and I settled for coffee.

"Maybe you can help me, Benji."

He munched thoughtfully and looked out the window but tilted his head toward me to tell me he was listening.

"You ever heard of a fella called Leo Nimzic?"

He nodded slowly and responded in a quiet tone that only I could hear over the sounds of people talking, plates clattering, the grill sizzling, and the order bell.

"Sure, I heard he's young and green but talented."

"His friend, Jesse Hunt, hired me to find him. It seems they were supposed to meet, and Leo never showed."

Benji stilled, keeping his gaze out the window. A few moments later, he swallowed with effort and turned shaken eyes on me.

"Listen, Anna," he urged quietly.

My pulse quickened when he used my name. *This must be serious.*

"You need to be careful. If Hunt hired you and you've already accepted the job, finish it quickly and move on."

I calmly prodded for more information. "Is there something I should know about Mr. Hunt?"

"If he's asking for help, give it to him. I mean it, Anna. Finish the job and get out."

I nodded to show I understood, knowing I wasn't going to get anything else about that.

"I heard Leo has an advisor in the coven since he's so young. Do you happen to know who that is?"

He thought for a moment, trying to overcome his ruffled emotions. He shook his head. "I've never even met someone from the Insebrog Coven. I only know about Leo because his age made him a topic of gossip. You're going to have to check the Registry."

I frowned at the prospect and glared at him. *Maybe I could ask Jesse to tell me who the advisor is.* "I'll manage."

Benji traced his inner wrist with his thumb, calling attention to the veins covered by thin skin. "You only have to ask," he suggested with a thick tone and heavy eyelids. "Would being tied to me be so bad? I'll make it fun for you."

I looked away uncomfortably. "I've never needed to access the Registry before, and I won't be indebted to anyone in that way."

After a heavy pause, I smirked and met his thoughtful gaze. "Do you know if there's a place where homosexuals in the magical community go to meet?"

That question returned us to our normal atmosphere.

"Why would I know that?"

"Well, can you find out? There's evidence that Leo went away with his male lover. I need to know who this fella is. Finding out where they met could help me figure it out."

Benji looked mortified at how searching for that information would look.

"Don't you love me anymore?" I teased.

"Sure, I do. How about some cash to fortify me?" He

leaned his face in, waiting for a kiss he knew wasn't coming.

"Bank's closed. Call Maggie when you find out. Won't you?" I stood to leave.

"I'll take a check then," he called after me playfully.

Back at the office, Maggie sat at her desk, typing something or other.

"Hey, Anna!" she greeted, smiling up at me.

"Good morning, Maggie. I'm just popping in to tell you to expect a message from Benji."

She smirked like she was going to enjoy yet another flirtatious battle.

"And could you call my dad and tell him you saw me alive?"

She looked at me keenly. "Oh, did you not go home last night, Anna?"

"I just slept at the office."

"Rhatz! I thought you'd finally found a fella."

"If you thought less about men and more about work, you might be a PI by now."

"Yeah, but where's the fun in that?"

I smiled and shook my head. "Just call my dad. Will ya?"

"Will do."

"Thanks, Maggie."

I watched her work for a moment. Maggie was the picture of a flapper. Her black hair was short with perfect finger waves, and she had the boyish frame that every woman envied. She was lively and wild, and she was my role model on how to fool others into thinking I was happy. *She lost her older brother in the war, but it's like she takes it as her personal mission to live twice as big for them both.*

I called Jesse on my office phone. His smooth voice made me forget about Benji's mysterious warnings.

"I have some updates if you'd like to meet later to hear them." *Can't risk talking about it over the phone. I never know who might be listening on the party line.*

"I'm available whenever you need me."

"I've got something to take care of this morning, but I can meet after."

"All right. If we need a quiet place, we can come to my apartment."

My heart skipped a beat at the thought of being alone at Jesse's. "That's fine," I answered, managing to keep my tone even. "Where is it?"

"I'll pick you up."

"Swell. Meet me at Lillian's at eleven."

"I'll be there."

ELEVEN

L illian was busy with another client when I arrived. To pass the time, I perused the many books on the shelves of her sitting room.

I opened the spell book closest to me. It was hand-bound in brown leather with the words "Morgan's Grimoire" etched into the spine. The rough parchment was thick but brittle. As I carefully turned the pages, I saw the book was organized by spell purpose *Interesting, but not particularly useful to humans.*

I carefully reshelved *Morgan's Grimoire* and skimmed for something else. A row of similarly-bound volumes caught my eyes. The candlelight danced on the gold letters embossed on the black leather, like flames beckoning travelers in the night. "The History of Witches and Witchcraft," the gold leaf declared. They were lined up in order from volumes one to eleven.

I chose volume eleven and cracked the stiff spine to a random page.

"After an investigation, ordered by the Council of Covens, they discovered that the spiritualist movement started when a witch born to human parents was not found in time to integrate her into witch society. Many of the other so-called mediums of the movement turned out to be frauds.

"However, it was the humans' response to the spiritualists that intrigued the Council. They seemed to be reacting in a less violent way than they had in the past. It was true some humans were angry or unsettled by the concepts presented by the spiritualists, but there did not seem to be any burnings on the horizon. Some on the Council believed humans were ready to accept witches, and we could finally come out of the shadows. Others were still afraid; the Burning Times felt fresh in their minds.

"In 1887, the Seybert Commission published their findings on Spiritualism. Their denunciation of mediumship upset many witches, though we knew the people they had investigated were frauds. But it was in 1888, when Margaret Fox admitted to participating in the elaborate hoax with her sisters, that witches began to panic.

"Many felt our chance to reveal ourselves was disappearing as humans began to believe the spiritualists debunked. However, it was the mediums who ultimately convinced the Council to come forward. Their case was the human frauds were dishonoring the spirits, and it was causing unrest in the Otherworld. The spirits demanded the misunderstanding be solved and threatened an uprising if it was not. After much discussion and divination, the Council decided the best way to appease the spirits and move forward as witchkind was to reveal ourselves to the humans."

Hearing Lillian exit the broom closet, I closed the book and reshelved it. She was accompanied by an elderly woman who appeared foggy with bliss.

"Peter looked well today. Didn't he?" the woman asked Lillian.

"I'm sure he did, Wendy," Lillian replied, escorting her to Starlight Avenue.

When Lillian returned, she led me back through the broom closet. I chose the water room.

The walls were a calming blue, and the bedspread was seaweed green. The lighting appeared as though we were underwater looking up as it rippled through the room in streaked rays.

Lillian gave me the usual spiel, and I agreed as I lay down and closed my eyes.

I waited impatiently outside the vaudeville turned movie theater. Rocking on my heels, I smoothed the skirt of my dark blue sailor dress. The warm breeze rustled the remaining orange leaves of the strangled, urban sidewalk trees. I searched the street for a familiar form. I'd promised myself today would be the day, but I was still nervous. A refined matron and her charge glared at me disapprovingly, no doubt believing me to be promiscuous for going to the movies. I stared back at them until they raised their noses at me.

While I'd been fighting a silent battle, Cy had dragged in. He heaved deep breaths, trying to recover from his niggle and wrapped an arm around his cramped stomach.

My heart didn't fail to skip a beat at the sight of him. He looked darb even though his lanky limbs had yet to fill out his shirt and vest. *I guess he's still growing like a weed.* He'd already grown to half a head taller than me in a few months. I couldn't help but stare at the ends of his golden hair, which curled around the brim of his brown newsboy hat. I bit my lip to stop myself from reaching for the soft tips.

"Sorry I'm late," he gasped, distracting me. "Mr. Wallace was watching me closely today. It's like he knew I was going to ditch my lesson."

"He probably did. Maybe if you were a better actor, he wouldn't have suspected you," I ragged.

"If I were a better actor, my mom wouldn't insist on his instruction. Where's Jack?" He looked around when he didn't see him.

"He couldn't make it," I lied smoothly, having practiced for this moment.

His blue eyes showed no suspicion as he nodded his acknowledgment.

Since the movie was starting soon, there were only two other people in line at the box office.

We purchased our tickets with feigned confidence, the best way to get into a show when just underage.

The theater was crowded, so we had to sit in the back. The projector already clicked above us as it played the newsreel. As the film informed us of the latest news from war-torn Europe, we watched the witch magically crank the projector in the balcony. He lazily spun his finger in a circle, making the arm turn without effort.

Another witch at the front of the stage organized a flute, a trumpet, a violin, and a piano. As he raised his arms, we saw he had a thin conductor's baton in each hand. He pointed one to the piano and the other at the violin. They started to play just as the title screen announced that *Carmen* was beginning.

We settled into the movie, but I couldn't relax. In the dark, hushed theater, I was all too aware of Cy's proximity. My heartbeat thundered in my ears, and I tried to control my breathing while my arm brushed against his. He didn't seem to notice.

I managed to pick up on the story even as my body hummed. As the men were completely enamored with Carmen, I looked at Cy sideways. He watched with rapt attention. *He seems captivated. Does he find Geraldine Farrar attractive? No, don't try to talk yourself out of it. You're finally going to tell him.*

As I admired Carmen's fierce, free spirit, I couldn't help but wish Cy looked at me the way Don José and Escamillo looked at Carmen.

She's so alluring as she smiles and acts coy. Maybe if I acted that way, Cy would reciprocate.

I took turns watching the movie and staring at Cy until Don José grabbed Carmen and told her she belonged to him. At that point, the lead up to the tragic ending monopolized my attention.

As the audience started to leave, Cy turned to me. I quickly wiped my tears.

He laughed. "Caill, are you crying?"

"Shut your yap," I sniffled.

"When do you have to be home?" he asked as we exited the theater.

"I've got time. You?"

He shook his head. "Mom has rehearsal for her show next week, so I'm on my own tonight."

"Does she still not approve of movies?"

"They are the death of theatre," he informed.

I laughed. "Let's go for a walk by the river," I suggested.

He shrugged in agreement.

"So what did you think of the movie?" I asked, trying to pluck up some nerve.

"I couldn't believe the men. She had them enthralled."

"Well, people will do anything for love."

He nodded as though he'd just learned a life lesson.

"Didn't you think she was beautiful? I mean, they all were. Don José and Escamillo were dead handsome, too," I hedged at the last minute.

He shrugged again. "I guess so. The sword fight was the best."

We stopped in the middle of the bridge and peered down into the murky river. We watched a yellow candy wrapper race fallen leaves toward the lake. Cy leaned his arms on the red painted guardrail of the bridge.

The breeze made the ends of Cy's hair flicker in the streetlamp light, like the bright edges of a flame.

I stared at him with intent until he noticed.

"What?"

I smiled at him, hoping he would catch my meaning without words.

He half smiled, half squinched. "What?"

"Cy, do you remember when we went to the circus?"

"How could I forget?" He turned to me and started to laugh. "Your hair turned blue."

I giggled with him. "Do you remember the fortune teller?"

His smile vanished, but he nodded.

"What did she tell you?" I asked.

"I don't remember exactly," he said, averting his eyes back to the river.

I moved closer to him and put my hand gently on his arm. He looked at me in surprise. "Did you notice a change in me after that day?" I pleaded for him to catch on.

His face scrunched in thought. "A change? I guess so. I just thought you were growing up. You started acting kind of girlie. I thought your aunt had finally gotten to you. But you'll always be Caill to me." He smiled as if trying to reassure a shortcoming.

I sighed.

His expression turned serious. "You don't have to say anything. I already know. I've always known."

My heart raced. "You do?"

He nodded.

"Well…What do you think about it?"

"Why would it affect me now? I said I've always known. It was just a matter of time. I'm happy for you both."

"What?"

"You and Jack. I'm glad you've finally realized your feelings for each other. Just don't forget who introduced you." He laughed awkwardly.

My eyes started to water. "You're a chump, Cyril Jenson," I choked.

Realizing I was crying, Cy's face paled. He shifted his weight from one foot to the other, unsure of what to do.

"I'm not in love with Jack. I'm in love with you."

He stilled, stunned, like I'd hit him over the head. "W-what? What about Jack?"

"What about him?"

"He—" He cut himself off. "You're in love with me?"

I nodded, wiping my tears and sniffing hard.

His shock eventually gave way to understanding. He smiled and laughed, rubbing his hand on the back of his neck. "Well, that explains a lot."

His laughter broke my tension. I stepped in close to him, resting my forehead on his shoulder and my fingertips on his chest. My heartbeat did a jig.

Pulling away slightly, I looked up into his blue eyes, dark in the night.

"I love you, Cyril Jenson," I whispered.

He traced my chin and jaw with his thumb. I looked into his eyes anxiously but was relieved to see he was pure Cy. This time, I welcomed his touch. Warmth spread through me, and my breath hitched in anticipation as he leaned toward me. He sealed my lips gently with his. The sweetness of our second kiss was quickly followed by the heat of our third.

TWELVE

I could still feel Cy's warm breath on my lips as I emerged from the Living Memory as if gently waking from a restful sleep.

I left the smear of a contented smile on my face while paying Lillian and following her out of the broom closet.

My cheeks warmed with guilt when I was greeted with a sight that made my heart pound. Jesse sat comfortably in the sitting room, his legs crossed at the knees, with a newspaper crossword puzzle in his lap. He loosely held a pencil in his hand, the tip of which rested on his full, lower lip. A shiver of desire ran through me when he met my eyes and gave me the smallest of smiles.

I don't know how long I would've stared speechless if Lillian hadn't put her hand on my shoulder. She smiled knowingly, a sparkle in her eyes. I turned away, shame clenching my stomach.

"It's nice to see you again, Jesse." Lillian smiled politely.

Jesse stood, folding the newspaper and slipping it into his coat pocket, and nodded at Lillian's greeting.

"Thank you again for recommending Ms. Caill to me, Lillian."

"Of course. I'm sure she'll be of great help to you."

"Are you ready to blouse?" Jesse asked me.

I nodded and told Lillian I'd see her again soon. Silently following Jesse to Starlight Avenue, I couldn't help but shiver again as I watched him whisper life into his cupped hands, creating our guide. His voice was soft and smooth when he performed magic. It caressed my ears like a warm spring breeze on freshly exposed skin. It seemed everything he did was elegant and alluring somehow. I thought of the men in *Carmen* and could easily see women doing anything for Jesse.

The violet will-o'-the-wisp led us to a large basement, which seemed to act as storage. I continued to tail Jesse when he entered a concrete stairwell. Our footsteps echoed as we climbed to the third floor.

We entered a hallway with industrial gray carpet and doors with tarnished brass numbers. Jesse's keys tinkled flatly as he pulled them out of his pocket and opened a door at the end of the hall labeled, "310."

"Make yourself at home," he suggested as he flicked on the light and removed his hat and overcoat. I hung my coat next to his on a hook near the door. His apartment was what one would expect from someone who didn't have much. The place opened into a living room, sparsely furnished with the type of tables and seats landlords bought in bulk to make their pre-furnished rentals pass-able. On the right, there was a short hall with two doors, no doubt leading to a bedroom and bathroom. Ahead was a bar with two stools, behind which was a small kitchen. The walls were a dingy white, the way walls look when someone who smokes like a chimney moves out and a thin coat of paint tries to cover the evidence. The only decoration was an unwound clock above the radio.

"How long have you lived here?"

He shrugged. "A year, maybe?"

He motioned for me to have a seat on either the divan or armchair as he continued on to the kitchen. I sat politely at the edge of the divan.

"I figured a private place would be best for you to tell me what you've learned so far," he explained as he tinkered around in the kitchen.

"Good idea."

Jesse returned with a plate of sandwiches and two cups of coffee. He placed them on the low table and sat beside me on the divan. *It doesn't seem like he's put much of himself in his living space, but he has food and there isn't any dust. He must spend quite a bit of time here but hasn't really made it his home.*

He nodded toward the offering. "We can eat here while you catch me up."

I nibbled at the ham and cheese sandwich and thanked him. As he took a bite of his sandwich, he looked at me expectantly.

"I spoke to one of Mr. Nimzic's neighbors. She said she saw him willingly leave his house and get into a motorcar around eight the night he disappeared."

Jesse furrowed his brow. "Was he with someone? Leo doesn't have a motorcar."

I nodded. "It seems he was intimate with the person he left with. The neighbor saw them necking and recognized his acquaintance as someone who has visited him before."

His eyes widened. "But I told you, Rose was on stage that night. Is he two-timing her with another woman? That doesn't seem like him."

"The person he left with wasn't a woman."

He looked bewildered at first then his sandwich dropped to the floor along with his jaw.

I analyzed his shocked expression for any signs of prior knowledge and found none. I sighed in relief. "I'm sorry to have shocked you. I take it you didn't know he also… enjoys men?"

Jesse covered his mouth with the back of his hand. "I had no idea," he mumbled, squinting his eyes in thought.

"It could be that his tryst with this man is the reason he's been acting so strange lately. Perhaps their romance is fairly recent, or he had mixed feelings about telling you."

He nodded. "But this still doesn't explain why he'd make plans with me and never show. Thank you for telling me, but please continue to look for him."

I nodded and quietly chewed my lunch. Jesse placed his dropped meal back on the plate and settled for his cup of joe. His eyes looked off into the distance as he thought about what I'd just told him.

I didn't want to be rude, but I couldn't help but stare at him. He didn't seem to notice, too preoccupied with his own thoughts.

Meeting my gaze suddenly, he asked, "How reliable do you think Leo's neighbor is?"

I tried to pretend I'd just looked his way when he'd spoken, but my face heated up.

His mouth twitched into a small smile.

I shivered and cleared my throat. "She seemed shaken by the sight of Mr. Nimzic and his lover together. I almost had to drag it out of her. I think she's reliable as far as what she observed."

Jesse frowned as if he'd wanted a different answer.

After finishing my sandwich, I pulled him from his thoughts. "I hear you are a member of Mr. Nimzic's coven. Can I assume you know who his advisor is?"

"Yes," he said without elaborating.

"I'd like to question him. Can you tell me his name and address?"

Jesse didn't respond for a moment as though he was weighing whether to give me the information. "I called him when Leo went missing. He doesn't know anything."

"Regardless, I'd like to speak with him myself."

"We aren't supposed to tell humans who's in the coven," he explained, the hesitation in his voice apparent. "His name is Patrick Sullivan."

"Do you have his address?"

"I'd like to accompany you on your visit. I can drive you there."

I thought about his offer for a moment. *I don't know Patrick Sullivan. Therefore, I can't tell whether he's more likely to spill if I'm with Jesse or alone. It may be easier if Jesse introduces us. I'm an outsider and a human he doesn't know, after all, and Jesse is a member of the coven.* I tried not to let my desire to be with Jesse longer have any weight in my decision. "That's probably a good idea," I told him. "He may be more comfortable with you there to introduce us."

"What're you hoping to learn from him?" he asked,

"Mr. Sullivan has a unique relationship with your friend. Mr. Nimzic may have told him about his mystery lover. He may have sought personal advice from him since he's a trusted advisor."

Jesse nodded. "It's possible." He smiled, and my heart jumped. "Let's go then."

We left Jesse's apartment and descended to the street instead of Starlight Avenue. Jesse opened the passenger door to a dark blue motorcar parked near the curb. I nodded my thanks and climbed in. He shut the door and walked around to sit behind the driver's wheel.

The sounds of the city couldn't compare to the deafening silence inside the motorcar. As I watched Jesse drive with a sort of fluid grace, Benji's warnings rang in my ears. *What do I know about Jesse Hunt?*

Separating my body's undesired reactions to him, I analyzed him as a small boy does a praying mantis.

I know he's close friends with Leo Nimzic, a young but talented high priest of an ancient coven. He seems to have lived in the area for about a year. I haven't seen him do much magic, but he is a witch. He knows Lillian somehow, at least enough for her to recommend me to him. Still, their interactions were polite rather than friendly. Benji knew him by name and warned me about him, but Benji knows a lot of people. I really don't know very much at all.

Though I was usually comfortable with silence, and I got the feeling Jesse was too, the quiet that sat between us seemed thick and unnatural.

"How did you and Mr. Nimzic meet?" I asked lightly.

"We met by chance. I'd just moved here, and I hadn't met many witches in the area yet. I spent a lot of time exploring the city since I didn't have friends to show me around. I stumbled upon this little café and stopped in for a cup of coffee. It was crowded, and I accidentally spilled my coffee on Leo when I bumped into him. He was very understanding and, after finding out I was new to town, even offered to buy me another cup."

"He sounds like a swell fella."

"He's the best," Jesse praised with a sad smile.

"You seem to know your way around town now."

"Yeah, Leo really took me in and introduced me to a lot of people."

"Is that how you met Lillian?"

He frowned a little. "No, Lillian is one of those people who seems to know everyone." He hesitated before continuing. "Rose sent me to her when I was having nightmares."

"Oh, so you're also friends with Mr. Nimzic's girlfriend?"

He nodded. "Rose was one of the first people I met when I moved here. I actually introduced her and Leo."

"It must be upsetting to know he's seeing someone else then."

He shook his head in disappointment. "I can't understand it, but there must be more to the story. I don't want to judge him too harshly before I know all the facts."

I admired his faith in his friend, but I couldn't help but be a little irritated on Rose's behalf.

"You said you've lived in your apartment for about a year? Where did you move from?"

"I've lived all kinds of places. I moved around a lot." He hedged the question, and I took the hint and stopped asking. It was another ten minutes before we reached Patrick Sullivan's large suburban home.

"Mr. Sullivan isn't connected to Starlight Avenue?" I asked as Jesse held out a hand to help me out of the motorcar.

For a reprehensible moment, I'd wished we weren't wearing gloves and that I could feel the warmth of his bare skin on mine.

"No, this is a quiet neighborhood, and Patrick runs a lending library. So it's not suspicious for many people to visit."

Mr. Sullivan's home was on the corner of a high-class street. His brick house was square with an observatory tower on the north side. His lawn, though brown with winter's sleep, was clear of fallen leaves. Three large trees' branches stretched their naked fingers in a web, which would shade his home come spring. A wrought iron fence, about seven feet tall and topped with elegant spikes, surrounded Mr. Sullivan's land. Though the fence warned intruders, the gate was unlocked. Its groan ended in a squeak when Jesse pushed it open.

We walked up the stone path and rang Mr. Sullivan's bell. After a few moments, a short man with white hair and sharp eyes answered the door.

Jesse gave him a polite smile, which he didn't return.

Undeterred, Jesse introduced us. "Patrick, this is Anna Caill. She's the private detective I've hired to find Leo."

Patrick stared at me hard, and he raised an eyebrow at Jesse.

"She comes highly recommended in the community." Jesse assured him that, though I was human, I was sympathetic toward witches.

I held out my hand. "I'm sorry we couldn't meet under more pleasant circumstances, Mr. Sullivan."

His eyes scrutinized me as if determining my competency. After a heavy pause, he nodded stiffly and shook my hand.

"I don't know where Leo is, but I will help if I can," he said in a serious tone.

Inviting us in, Patrick led us through his echoing foyer with the shuffling gait of advanced age.

We entered a well-stocked library with armchairs near reading lamps and smooth tables with wooden chairs. A spiral staircase led to a catwalk, which gave access to the upper shelves.

Patrick stopped and turned to Jesse. "Stay here," he instructed. "Ms. Caill, follow me."

Jesse opened his mouth to protest, but a sharp look from Patrick silenced him. Jesse's lips flattened into an angry line, but he didn't say anything.

I followed Patrick to a door in the corner of the library. He unlocked it with an intricate key and motioned for me to enter.

The windowless room held shelves of tattered, old books. A small, round table with two wooden chairs was illuminated by a reading lamp. Patrick and I each took a seat at the table.

"How may I help you?" Patrick asked in a serious tone while lacing his hands on the table in front of him.

"Do you know what led to Mr. Hunt hiring me?"

He nodded. "Leo was to meet Jesse to talk with him. Jesse called me that night wondering if I knew where Leo was. He claims Leo never showed."

There was a hint of disbelief in Patrick's tone.

"You believe Mr. Nimzic did meet Mr. Hunt as planned?"

"I believe Leo was going to deliver unwelcome news to Jesse, and I believe I couldn't find Leo by scrying for him. How much do you know about magic, Ms. Caill?"

"Not much."

"Scrying is a spell, which can be used to find lost people or things. Like all magic, the witch performing the spell needs to have a talent for that type of spell-work. While I'm not a master, I'm usually successful when scrying. Either Leo doesn't want to be found, or someone is cloaking his location. I'm still working on a way to find him without going to the Registry. You appear to be an honest young woman, even if you are human. If Jesse has something to do with Leo's disappearance, I don't believe you know about it."

"Why would Mr. Hunt hire me if he had something to do with Mr. Nimzic's disappearance?"

"The Council of Covens' punishment for harming another witch, especially a high priest, is severe. Multiple people knew Leo was going to meet Jesse. If he was the last to see him, that would implicate him. Hiring you redirects suspicion."

I nodded at his sound reasoning. "Mr. Sullivan, are you aware of Mr. Nimzic's romantic involvements?"

"I know he worships some singer Jesse introduced him to, but I've never met her." He waved his hand dismissively.

"Did you notice Mr. Nimzic acting strangely as of late?"

"The boy is under a lot of pressure. Truth be told, his magic isn't advanced enough yet for him to lead a large coven effectively. I noticed he was showing signs of stress, which is why I urged him to choose a successor."

My eyebrows raised in surprise. "It's my understanding that Mr. Nimzic is still quite young. Isn't it too early for him to name a successor?"

"He is young, but naming a successor doesn't merely ensure the lineage of the coven. It also strengthens and stabilizes the high priest's magic. The successor is the only witch who can provide direct support to the high priest. Appointing a successor also ensures the safety of the coven's relics, which automatically change ownership upon the high priest's death. Otherwise, the relics are effectively lost."

"Mr. Sullivan, you said Mr. Nimzic was to meet Mr. Hunt to deliver unwelcome news. Can you tell me what that news was?"

Patrick chewed on his lower lip. "I really shouldn't discuss coven business, but in light of the current circumstances...Leo had two candidates he was considering as his successor. He was to meet Jesse to inform him that he was choosing the other."

"Mr. Hunt was a candidate for the next high priest of your coven?"

Patrick nodded.

"And Mr. Nimzic chose someone else? May I know whom?"

Patrick pulled a scrap of paper and a pencil near the lamp toward him and wrote something. He handed the paper to me. It had an address on it.

"Her name is Elizabeth Shelton. She attends school during the day, so visit her in the evening."

I nodded and pocketed the information. "Mr. Sullivan, do you know of any blond men Mr. Nimzic may be close with?"

He blinked in confusion. "There are a few members of the coven who have blond hair, but no one he's particularly close with."

"This would be a fairly recent acquaintance I think."

He shook his head. "Why do you ask?"

"His neighbor has seen a man of that description visiting him recently, but no one seems to know who he is." *I don't think Patrick needs to know the details.* "How familiar are you with Mr. Nimzic's schedule on the day of his disappearance?"

"As far as I know, Leo was to meet Elizabeth then Jesse."

I stood from the table and passed Patrick one of my calling cards. "You will let me know if you learn any more information?"

He nodded and stood. "Yes, and please tell me if there's anything else I can do."

"I will, and don't worry. I'll find Mr. Nimzic."

"Thank you."

When we returned to the library, Jesse stood from the armchair he'd been sitting in. His face and demeanor were smooth and cool, but his mouth was pressed into a line.

Patrick showed us to the door. We shook hands and said our goodbyes.

As we drove away from Patrick's, I asked Jesse if he would drop me off at my office. He nodded but didn't speak.

After a while, he interrupted the silence and my thoughts. "Was Patrick of any help?"

"Yes, he may have told me who the last person to see Mr. Nimzic was."

"And who's that?"

"Miss Elizabeth Shelton."

He nodded at the name he recognized. "Is that all he said?"

I hesitated to divulge all of Patrick's suspicions or his attempts to find Leo. "He didn't know much else. He'd never heard of his mysterious lover. He was convinced Mr. Nimzic only had eyes for Rose."

Jesse's gaze flicked to my face as if he knew I was leaving something out. "It seems we're all surprised by Leo's relationship."

"Well, maybe Rose or Miss Shelton can shed some light on the subject."

"Would you like me to accompany you when you visit them?"

"I heard The Black Moon can be difficult for humans to get into, so your help would be appreciated when I visit Rose tonight. As for Miss Shelton, I think I should visit her alone."

"You'll keep me apprised of any relevant information you learn from her?"

"Of course."

Once we arrived at my office building, we agreed to meet at The Black Moon at six.

THIRTEEN

Maggie looked up from the filing cabinets when I entered. "Hey, Anna," Maggie greeted, somewhat subdued.

"Hello, Maggie. Any messages?"

"Yeah, Jack called. It seems he has the information you requested, and he wants you to meet him tomorrow at eleven at Marchdale's."

"Thanks. I'm sorry to have you here, waiting for messages, on a Saturday. You can head out early."

Her eyes lit up at the possibilities. "Thanks, Anna! See you Monday."

I looked at the clock above the door she'd rushed out. I had a while before I needed to leave for The Black Moon. I sighed. *I guess it's time.*

I locked the door and walked a few blocks to the Cherry Street Metropolitan Police Station. I stood outside the square brick building, staring up at the blocked letters etched above the door. Taking a deep breath, I straightened my spine and strode in with purpose.

The place was in chaos as coppers pushed reluctant

people along to get their photographs taken and fill out paperwork.

"Move along, Damned." One cop shoved a handcuffed young man.

"I ain't done nothin'," he argued, stumbling to catch his balance.

I tried to maintain a stone-faced mask, but I couldn't stop my tongue from clicking as I watched how the coppers treated the witches. *There's nothing you can do about it. Just sneak through and try not to be noticed.*

Unfortunately, the desk sergeant looked up from his logbook just as I passed by.

His mean face split into a toothy grin. "Well, if it ain't little miss detective. Found any lost puppies lately? Hey, Baker! Look who's here."

Another glorified desk clerk looked up from his paperwork and leered at me. "Hey, Sweetheart, if you want a dick so bad, I've got one you can handle."

I smirked. "I would if there was anything to grab onto, Baker."

The coppers and their charges within earshot laughed as Baker reddened with anger.

I turned my back on him and walked farther into the bullpen, ignoring the whistles and kissing sounds that followed me.

At a door labeled "Detective Albert Hartley," I knocked and entered when a gruff voice called.

As I closed the door behind me, a balding man in his early fifties looked up from his desk. His dark, tired eyes crinkled as he smiled with a cigar clutched between his teeth.

I smiled back at Dad's old friend as he stood to embrace me.

"Anna, it's been a while. Did the boys give you a hard time?"

"Nothing I can't handle. By the way, what's with the scene out there? Why so many people?"

He frowned and sighed. "We found a coven holding a ritual in the park at dawn. I wish they'd stick to private places."

"What will happen to them?"

"They'll be booked, and the charges will probably be dropped. The city's got too much to worry about to prosecute people chanting while holding hands."

The solace I felt was minor since I knew what kind of abuse they'd have to take before they were released.

"So what brings you here? I can't imagine it's to see my ugly mug." He grinned.

I chuckled at him as I took a seat. "I wish it were. I'm working a missing person's case."

"And you want me to check the records to see if your fella fell in with a bad sort?"

"Would you?"

The end of his cigar glowed as he pulled on it; he let the smoke billow from his mouth. He nodded. "Who's the fella?"

"His name is Leo Nimzic. The case seems pretty straight-forward."

"Then why do you got that uneasy look?"

I bit my lip. "His neighbor saw him with someone no one else seems to know. Also, his friend couldn't find him even with magic."

"So what's your hunch? The Druzina?"

"I don't think it's that serious, but I'm here just to make sure."

He nodded solemnly and wrote a quick note. "All right,

I'll check our records and files on The Druzina to see what I can dig up."

I stood to go. "Thanks, Ace."

"Anytime. Hey, how's your dad doing?"

"About the same."

He shook his head sadly. "Give him my best."

"Will do," I said, crossing the room.

As I reached for the doorknob, he stopped me. "What are you doing for the holidays?"

I turned toward him and shrugged.

"Henry is coming to visit. Why don't you stop by? I know Frances would be glad to see you."

"Ace, are you still trying to set me up with your son again?" I chided. "You know we aren't interested in each other."

"You can't blame a fella for trying. We want to see him settled. You've got a good head on your shoulders, not like these girls he runs around with."

"He'll figure it out."

He grunted, and I laughed. "My regards to Frances and Henry. I'll talk to you later."

The whistles and jeers that followed me out came to an abrupt halt when Ace stuck his head out of his office door. I smiled over my shoulder at him and waved goodbye.

I took a deep breath of cold, fresh air when I stepped outside. Letting it out all at once, I let go of my nervous frustration at having to deal with the coppers. I hopped the nearest streetcar to the address Jesse had given me.

The Black Moon was a private club that seemed to skirt the law by exploiting loopholes. Because it was private, they couldn't be charged for performing magic in public. Since it was technically only opened to witches, no humans were corrupted by witnessing such ungodly acts.

Of course, the truth of the matter was the owner

frequently greased the palms of some big cheese. As long as they kept their heads down and didn't allow any loud-mouthed humans in, they could stay in business.

Jesse met me outside the converted warehouse that was The Black Moon. There was no business sign on the building, just an unobtrusive stone slab built into the corner with the address etched into it.

The side-door entrance led to a small room with only a man in a chair listening to whangdoodle on the radio next to him. He looked up at us as we entered, easily recognized Jesse as a fellow witch, and let us pass through the door at the other end.

I guess knowing the right people really can get you in anywhere. He barely glanced at me.

We entered a large room with a bar at one end and a stage at the other. In between were tables and chairs, still empty due to the early hour.

On the far left, there was a staircase leading to the second floor, where there were private meeting rooms in which illegal activity certainly never occurred.

A hostess with a short skirt and rolled down stockings greeted us with a too bright smile. "Here to get a drink before the show?" she asked.

"No, we're here to see Rose," Jesse explained.

The hostess frowned a little. "I'm sorry, Sir. Patrons aren't allowed backstage without an invitation."

The bartender looked up from wiping glasses at the hostess' apologetic tone. "He's a friend of Rose's, Grace," he told the hostess when he recognized Jesse.

Grace went red behind her rouge. "I'm sorry. I didn't know. I'm new."

Jesse gave her an understanding smile. "It's fine. Grace, was it? Good luck in your new job."

She beamed at him and sighed a little too contentedly. "Thanks."

Jesse waved at the bartender while I tried to ignore the sparkle in Grace's eyes as they clung to Jesse.

I followed Jesse into a small hallway at the right of the stage. There were four doors on the right side and one at the end of the hall. Jesse knocked and slowly opened the second door.

I heard an excited woman's voice. "Jesse," she said his name with a sweet smile that made my teeth hurt.

Her smile didn't slip as I entered the room behind him, but she stopped her approach.

"Rose," Jesse started in an explanatory tone. "This is Anna Caill. She's the private detective I've hired to find Leo."

She sneered at me, straightening her spine and sizing me up the way women do to each other. She wore a short, green dress and green satin dance shoes. Her blonde hair glittered like the golden threads you read about in fairy tales, the kind an evil dwarf spins in exchange for your unborn child.

"Ya don't say. A female dick. Well, I guess ya can see anythin' these days," she remarked offhandedly like she was watching a particularly unentertaining flea circus.

She turned her back on me and went to sit in front of the mirror of her dressing table. After picking up her cosmetics brush, she began applying a hint of glitter to her cheekbones.

I'd heard comments like that so many times that they barely even registered with me anymore, although it was unusual for a witch to say since women often held positions of power in the magical community.

"I'm here to ask you a few questions that may help me find Mr. Nimzic."

She didn't respond.

"Rose, I'm worried about Leo. You'll tell us what you know. Won't you?" Jesse encouraged.

She sighed. "I was hea' the night Leo was suppose' to meet Jesse. He neva' showed."

"When's the last time you saw or talked to him?"

She bit her lip and stood from the dressing table. After pacing to the far end of the room, she looked back at Jesse, who nodded.

She blew out a breath from pouting lips. "It's been a few weeks. We were on a break."

"What?" Jesse snapped. "You didn't tell me that."

Rose bit her lip at Jesse's reaction. "He'd been actin' strange, but I thought he was jus' workin' through somethin'. I knew he'd come back to me."

"Rose, are you aware Mr. Nimzic has another lover?"

Rose froze. "That's impossible." Her lack of expression gave nothing away.

"There's a witness who saw him with another man."

Rose's lips curled in disgust. "I haven't heard from him since we broke up, an' I don't know nothin' about who else he's been seein'."

With a tone of finality, she turned back to her mirror and resumed her preparations for going on stage. As she whispered something under her breath, two delicate, iridescent wings grew from between her shoulder blades. She turned her back to the mirror and looked over her shoulder to see if her prop wings were on straight.

"One more question: do you know anything about Mr. Nimzic's broken seal?"

She stilled her costume adjustments for a moment then looked at Jesse and me in the mirror. "No."

"All right," I nodded. "Well, please let me know if you think of anything that may be helpful to my investigation."

She ignored me, so I waved a calling card and placed it on a table near the door.

"I'll let you know when we find Leo," Jesse promised as he followed me out.

"I want to talk to the bartender about whether he's seen Mr. Nimzic recently," I told Jesse.

He nodded and then stopped as though he'd forgotten something. "I'll meet you at the bar in a second." He turned back toward Rose's dressing room.

The bartender corroborated Rose's story and said he hadn't seen Leo in a few weeks. His tone and the way he leaned toward me on the bar told me he was more than willing to cooperate with my investigation. Curious as to what was keeping Jesse, I quietly moved toward Rose's dressing room, stopping shy of the threshold.

"I've neva' seen it befoa'," Rose vowed.

"Don't lie to me, Rose. I won't be angry if you tell me the truth. Is this yours? If Leo broke up with you, I can understand why you'd use it."

"I ain't neva' had to use such tactics befoa'," Rose protested, affronted.

"All right, all right, I get it," Jesse soothed.

There was a short pause.

"Not now," Jesse warned.

"Come on," Rose pouted.

"No," he said firmly.

Feeling their conversation coming to a close, I quickly returned to the bar to wait for Jesse.

FOURTEEN

"Ready?" I asked Jesse when he met me at the bar.
He tilted his head slightly and squinted. I smiled politely.

"Yeah, do you want a ride home?"

"A lift back to my office would be swell."

"You aren't going home yet?"

"I still have some things to take care of," I lied.

The motorcar ride was quiet as I thought about the conversation I'd overheard.

As we pulled up to the curb, Jesse turned to me in the dim light and asked, "Are you all right?"

I was surprised by the concern in his voice. "I'm just thinking about the case." I brushed him off.

"I'm sorry Rose wasn't more helpful."

"On the contrary. She gave me oodles to consider. For instance, if Mr. Nimzic is as honorable as you say, he probably wasn't two-timing Rose. That means he didn't start dating his mystery lover until a few weeks ago when he and Rose broke up. Having a timeline could prove to be beneficial." *Still, Rose did seem to be hiding something. Did she suspect*

Leo had another lover? She seemed confident he would come back, and she didn't appear worried or upset when she found out. And what exactly were she and Jesse talking about?

"That's right around the time I started to notice Leo acting strangely," Jesse pointed out.

"That supports my conclusion."

"I'm going to see Miss Shelton tomorrow afternoon. I'll contact you after."

He nodded. "I'll be home, awaiting your call."

My heart jumped at the thought, and I scolded myself. *He'll be waiting to hear about the case.*

After saying goodnight, I went to my office. As I lay on the couch, the adrenaline that accompanied the fear of which memory I was about to relive couldn't stop exhaustion from overtaking me.

Stretched out on the rumpled sheets of Cy's bed, I lay on his chest in one of his shirts. He lazily stroked my naked hip and thigh as I smiled contentedly.

"That can't be good," I commented as he held up another tarot card from the deck beside him.

As humans, we couldn't use them for divination, but we often played card games with them. Still, Cy had memorized all their meanings.

The card he held showed a black knight on a white horse.

His chest vibrated as he chuckled. "It doesn't necessarily mean actual death," he explained. "It could represent the ending of anything, but with all endings come new beginnings."

I looked up into his blue eyes and love-tousled hair.

"Well, aren't you just full of wisdom." I smiled and kissed his bare chest.

His warm skin beneath my lips quickened my pulse in preparation for another round of lovemaking. He stilled my drifting hand, signifying he wasn't yet ready.

I pouted, and he kissed the top of my head to placate me.

"You're greedy," he tsked with a grin.

"Only with you," I countered, settling back onto his chest.

He pulled another card from the deck and showed it to me. A man smiled as he hung upside down by one foot.

"What does that one mean?" I asked.

"This fella has an interesting story. He travels the world in search of knowledge and wisdom. He even sacrificed an eye to take a drink from the well of destiny. In this card, he's hanging from the world tree, which grows from the well."

"That's dedication."

He stared at the card seriously. After a quiet moment, he said, "Take this card home with you."

"What? Why?"

"I admire what the hanged man stands for, and that's how I want you to see me."

"But if I take it, you won't have a full deck."

"That's all right. I just want you to think of me while I'm gone."

I propped myself up on my elbow and looked at him. "What do you mean while you're gone?"

He stared at the card as he continued. "I've decided to enlist."

Alarm shot through me, and I quickly sat up. "What? But you're only eighteen. I thought you had to be twenty-one."

"You can join at eighteen with parental consent."

"And your parents agreed? I thought they wanted you to be an actor?"

"You know they let me do whatever I want. Besides, my mother thinks being a war hero will boost my career when I return."

"But what if you don't come back?" I protested. "Men are dying, Cy."

He finally met my gaze. "You think I'm going to let those Huns get me?"

The challenge in his eyes made me reconsider my approach. "At least talk to Jack before you decide. He always has a unique perspective."

"Jack already knows. He was going to sign up with me, but his parents wouldn't allow it." Swallowing my initial shock, I sighed. *At least they aren't both going.*

But the consolation that Jack was staying didn't lessen the weight in my heart. Cy sat up and gently grabbed my chin.

"Please, Caill. I need to know my girl back home believes and takes pride in me. Can you do that for a lonely doughboy?"

My vision blurred and my nose stung. "You better come back to me, Cyril Jenson," my thick voice demanded.

He smiled gently. "Don't forget me," he whispered as he kissed my tears.

FIFTEEN

No gentle kisses erased the tears from my cheeks as the cold winter sun lit up my eyelids.

Heartache—my devoted companion—embraced me tightly as though we hadn't seen each other in years.

Like a mechanical wind-up doll, I got washed and changed for the day ahead. I put on my coat and hat to go see Lillian.

Before heading out, I called Dad. He answered almost immediately.

"Hello?"

"Dad, it's me. I'm just calling to check in."

"Anna, my girl, how's the investigation going? Have you found your missing fellow?"

"Not yet, but I still have a few leads to track down. I'm going to meet Jack this morning. It sounds like he might have something for me."

"Leave it to Jackie Boy to come through."

"Yeah, well I probably won't be home again tonight."

"Remember what I taught you, and good luck."

"Thanks, Dad. I love you."

"I love you too, my girl."

The sky was a clear blue, and the sun was bright but gave no heat as I ankled through the empty Sunday streets to Starlight Avenue.

Lillian was reading while enjoying a fragrant cup of tea when I entered her sitting room. She didn't look up right away but finished her page before marking it and putting the book on a side table. Finally, she met my eyes with a stern look. My brow furrowed in surprise.

"How long have you been coming to see me, Anna?"

I thought about it. "Six or seven years."

She nodded. "That's right, and have you noticed anything different about the last few days?"

My eyebrows drew together. "Not particularly. I've seen you every day as of late, but I always come to you more frequently when I'm working a case."

"Yes, but this time is different still."

"How so?" I asked, not quite sure I wanted to know but positive she wanted to tell me.

"Before, you were using Living Memory as a tool to maintain your everyday life and your relationships with friends and family."

"And now?"

"Now, you seem desperate, as if using it as a shield to separate yourself from others."

I pursed my lips and squinted at her accusations. "What would you have me do?" I spat, *and who do you think you are to tell me how to live my life?*

She sighed, shaking her head. "Just remember you are doing this for the living not the dead."

I swallowed my retort and nodded stiffly. "I don't have a specific memory today, but I'd like to use the Earth room." My tone was all business.

"Very well," Lillian replied distantly. She led me through the broom closet to the Earth room.

The walls and ceiling gave the impression of being in a thick forest. The trees' painted limbs stretched out above the bed of green moss, and leaves danced around the room as if blown by a gentle breeze. The sounds of birds singing in the distance completed the façade.

I climbed into the bed and accepted Lillian's disclaimer. Rather than picturing a place or time in my mind, I simply closed my eyes and whispered, "I want to see my soulmate."

I stared at the sad, decrepit mansion from outside the gate. The overgrown ivy strangled the paint off in flakes, and only one window at the very top wasn't cracked.

I shrank back from the thought of entering such a desolate and neglected place.

"We can do something else if you want," Jack suggested gently, placing a comforting hand on my shoulder.

"Don't baby her, Jack. She's brave enough. Or, are you the one who's scared?" Cy challenged.

"I'm not babying her. I just don't want her to be uncomfortable," Jack argued.

"Uncomfortable? That's the point of going to a haunted house." Cy laughed.

Their familiar bickering reassured me and gave me the courage to grab the iron gate. The metal burned my hand in the cold November night as I pushed it open.

Stepping onto the broken cobbled path, we tried to avoid the roots and the stones they'd pushed up.

On a creaky, crooked porch, an old woman with tightly-bound, white hair sat in a wicker chair. She didn't smile as we approached but nodded and stood with effort to meet us.

"On Samhain night, where the sun is fifteen degrees in Scorpio and the veil is thin, the spirits of the dead wander the world of the living. Like the people they once were, some of these spirits are violent and mean. Witches use lures to draw these malevolent spirits to desolate places and wards to keep them from leaving until they return to the Otherworld. This is one of those places. Do you under-stand the risks and enter of your own free will?" she asked in a tired, raspy voice.

We nodded and paid the entrance fee.

After pulling three tied cords with a metal charm on each from the basket at her feet, she handed them to us individually.

"Place these around your necks. Do not remove them until you come back here. They will protect you so far as no spirit may enter or touch your body."

She reached down again and handed each of us a lit lantern.

"Enter at your own risk," she finished, pointing to thick, wooden double doors with iron knockers and tarnished handles.

I looked at Cy, who grinned in anticipation. "Let's go," he urged, reaching for the door.

I didn't want to look like a coward, and I knew Cy had been looking forward to contacting real spirits. Still, my every instinct told me not to go into that house.

As he pushed open the door, it groaned as if it were in pain, shattering the palatable silence. I shivered and backed away, bumping into Jack.

"It's all right," he whispered. "I'm here with you, and we can leave any time you want."

I opened my mouth to say I already wanted to leave. But as Cy stepped into the house and out of sight, I rushed to catch up to him.

The entrance hall could've once been called grand. Now, the wallpaper was peeling, the floor was covered in recently disturbed dust, and the staircase was caved in on one side. The high ceiling made me feel exposed, and I looked around frantically for any sign of spirits. All was unnaturally quiet and still.

Cy didn't seem discouraged in his quest. He forged ahead, and Jack and I had to run to keep up.

"Don't go so fast," Jack complained when I fell behind their longer strides.

Cy scowled at him but showed no indication of slowing. Jack matched my pace as we entered a dark, dusty sitting room. What used to be white sheets covered spindle-legged couches and chairs.

We passed through to a music room. I stared at the piano nervously, expecting it to hammer an out-of-tune note without warning. The fact that it sat quietly didn't lessen my anxiety.

Entering our third room with no sign of ghosts, Cy pressed his lips in disappointment. He slowed his pace and frowned in the lantern light.

Just as I'd started to relax, we heard clear footsteps above us. I jumped and gasped at the sudden sound, but Cy flew from the room toward the grand staircase.

"Cy, wait for us!" I called after him, but he didn't listen.

"Don't worry," Jack said at my side. "You know how he is about anything having to do with magic or witches. We'll catch up to him at our own speed."

I nodded at Jack, and we headed back to the staircase to follow Cy.

Carefully climbing around the hole in the staircase, we slowly moved in the direction we'd heard the footsteps.

Entering a bedroom with a four-poster bed and a fireplace, the temperature suddenly dropped. I hugged myself with my arm that wasn't holding the lantern. Eyeing the drafty fireplace, I turned to leave.

A loud thump behind me ripped a scream from my throat before I could clamp my lips shut. I dropped my lantern, and the flame went out when the glass shattered on the floor.

Frozen in place, I hadn't realized I was shivering until Jack wrapped his arms around me.

"It's all right," he soothed. "It was only a candlestick falling from the mantle."

He continued to shush me and gently stroked my hair as I clenched my eyes shut and buried my face in his chest. Enveloped in his warm embrace, with my nose filled with his familiar scent, my body melted into his. After I'd calmed, he pulled away slightly and looked down at me.

"Let's get Cy and leave. What do you say? I'll buy you a slice of pumpkin pie and a glass of warm apple cider. Doesn't that sound good?"

I nodded and smiled at him. He picked up his lantern from the floor beside us and took my hand in his, leading me from the room.

"Cy?" Jack called as we continued down a hallway lined in recently disturbed cobwebs.

Eventually, we heard the timbre of Cy's voice, though I couldn't make out what he was saying. We followed the sound to a set of closed, frosted French doors.

Jack handed me the lamp and tried to pull the door open. When the door wouldn't budge, he let go of my hand to give it his full strength.

"Cy?" he called, but Cy didn't respond.

Finally, Cy's voice went silent, and there were sounds of a struggle. We heard bumps and crashes, and Jack doubled his efforts to open the door. After a moment, the struggle ceased, and both doors opened on their own.

Cy stood in front of a dark wooden desk, smirking at us with bright eyes. Blood dripped lazily from a scratch on his cheek, but he seemed unconcerned.

"Cy, let's go," Jack urged. "We don't want to be here anymore."

A winking of light reflecting off metal on the floor caught my eye, and I bent to pick it up. It was the necklace the witch outside had given Cy.

"Jack," I gasped, showing him the necklace.

He looked at it, and we both stared at Cy.

"Cy…?" I asked.

His smirk widened. "Guess again," he chuckled playfully.

"Get out of our friend!" Jack demanded.

The unknown spirit laughed. "Why should I? It's been a while since I've been corporeal."

"Please," I begged, tears filling my eyes. "Please, let Cy go."

Not-Cy's smirk softened, and he sauntered toward me.

"What a wonderful expression you're making, like a flower with raindrops on its silky petals. I wish I would have found you before this eager boy. It would be so much more fun to be inside you. What do you say? Will you take off that charm and let me in?"

"Absolutely not," Jack answered for me.

The spirit didn't acknowledge Jack but grabbed my chin and forced me to look at him. From the corner of my eye, I saw our reflection in a cracked mirror. Though I was staring at Cy's blond hair and blue eyes, the man in the reflection looked completely different. He was handsome in a dangerously mysterious way with slicked back, black hair and a dark enticing smile. I stiffened as his breath caressed my face.

"Don't touch her," Jack snarled, grabbing Not-Cy's wrist.

With a flick, he sent Jack flying across the room. Pinned to the wall by an invisible force, Jack struggled to free himself.

Unconcerned, Not-Cy turned his full attention back to me. "I'll tell you what. I only get a short while in this world every year, and it's been a long time since I've felt what it is to be human. If you give me a kiss, I will let your friends go." He smiled seductively.

"Leave her alone," Jack yelled helplessly.

"I know you like this boy. I can tell by how you look at him. He's an idiot for not knowing," he added in a whisper.

I frowned and tried to look away, but he held my chin immovable. *This isn't how I wanted to tell Cy I love him.*

"You're not ready to confess? That works for me just fine. We can keep this between the two of us. Cy here need never know."

"If I do this, you'll let Cy and Jack go and allow us to leave in peace?"

He smiled, ready to make a deal. "You have my word."

"Fine," I agreed.

"Anna, no," Jack protested.

"It's the easiest way to help you and Cy, Jack."

"She's right, Jack. Exorcisms can be quite painful for the host after all."

Not-Cy stepped close to me, wrapping an arm around my waist and pressing me to him. Jack grunted as he continued to struggle against his bonds.

Looking into Cy's too bright eyes, I steeled myself. *It's still Cy. It's Cy's body, and Cy is in there somewhere.*

My stomach flopped unpleasantly no matter what I told myself.

"Don't be so stiff, and give me that look I like so much," The ghost urged pleasantly.

I tilted my face up toward him and resigned myself. He frowned slightly at my expression.

Leaning in, he placed his lips to my ear and whispered, "I want you to remember your first kiss will never be with your beloved."

Tears stung my eyes again, and he sighed into a satisfied smile. "There it is."

His lips were soft at first then passionate as he pressed me to him. I took it like a martyr, telling myself it was all for Cy and Jack.

I knew when the spirit had kept his word and left because Cy's limbs went limp, and Jack crashed to the floor. I tried to support Cy's weight before he hit the floor, but he was taller than me. I managed to keep him upright long enough for Jack to drag him to a nearby chair.

I put the necklace around his neck and stood, turning my back to Jack's upset expression.

"We'll have to wait until Cy wakes. I don't think we can get him outside by ourselves," I said, trying to keep a steady voice.

Jack didn't respond but wrapped his comforting arms around me from behind. The moment I felt his warmth, I sagged into him, letting him support my weight.

He held me as I cried out my despair, keeping me together with quiet strength until I finished. Finally, he turned me around and wiped my wet cheeks.

"Thank you, Anna. You saved us," he praised, knowing

exactly what I needed to hear. "If it weren't for your brav-ery, who knows what would've happened."

He gently ran his thumb over my lower lip, trying to hide his sorrow. "Your kisses are yours to give, Anna. That one may have just saved our lives."

"You're right." I nodded. "It's a small price to pay for your and Cy's safety. Thank you, Jack. You always know how to make it better." I smiled up at him and kissed him on the cheek.

Leaving Jack's embrace, I returned to Cy and sat on the arm of the chair in which he slept. As I affectionately stroked his hair, I made myself a promise. *It's time. I'm going to tell Cy how I really feel no matter what.*

SIXTEEN

Whenever I let my subconscious choose which memory to relive, there was always a risk it may choose a bittersweet one. My feeling of contentment wasn't nearly as strong when I squinted my eyes open, but seeing Cy still eased the knot in my gut.

I didn't promise to see Lillian the following day, though I knew I would. I didn't want her to frown or nag at me. I simply handed over the kale and put on my shoes, hat, and coat.

As soon as I left Starlight Avenue, I hailed a dimbox to Marchdale's Rifle Club. The edifice of the club exemplified the image of gentry at leisure. The building was imposing but dignified. The grounds and interior provided a relaxing atmosphere to shoot, play sports, drink, read, smoke, or anything else its paying members did for pleasure.

It was a place where working-class people like Jack and I stuck out in an unpleasant way. They tolerated Jack's presence because he was an excellent marksman. He was the man to beat, and he kept their ranking top notch in competitions with other clubs. They would accept him until someone better came along, but Jack didn't seem to mind. So long as he had a rifle range to practice at, he was content to be left alone by The Darbs.

A polite yet stiff doorman opened the door for me as I entered. I smiled into his bland face.

"I'm here to meet Jack O'Keefe," I informed him.

"Mr. O'Keefe is at the indoor range," he replied in an uninterested manner.

"Thank you."

He didn't acknowledge my gratitude.

I hadn't been there often, but I remembered the way to the range. The maroon-rugged halls silenced the sound of my heels as I passed by the quiet reading rooms. The game rooms seemed to have more activity. Two young men with clinchers hanging from their lips looked up from their game of billiards, eyeing me with appreciation as I hoofed through the room. I ignored their invitation to a drink of scotch.

At the back of the building, past the indoor badminton court, was the indoor rifle range. To muffle the sound of shots fired, the stone walls were padded with tapestries of men on horses chasing their hounds.

Jack knelt with his rifle pointed at one of ten paper targets. The only other occupant was a teenage boy, who stood by to assist.

Jack didn't look up when I entered, and I quietly leaned on the wall behind him.

His shot fired, killing the paper with ease and accuracy. As Jack dropped his arms, I whistled to get his attention before he reloaded. He looked over his shoulder and smiled at me. All the tension I'd carried around in my limbs left with his familiar warmth.

Looking at the teenage boy, Jack tilted his head toward

the target. The boy ran to the end of the range to retrieve it. As he returned, Jack handed him the rifle.

"Ask Williams to bring two cups of coffee to reading room three. Will you, Teddy?"

"Yes, Sir."

Jack smiled and patted the boy's shoulder. "Thanks."

As Teddy scurried away, Jack held out his arm to me. I smiled and took it, letting him lead the way.

The door of reading room three had a sign labeled, "Reserved." The room felt cozy, with two armchairs, a reading lamp in between, and a low table. Jack's bag sat beside one of the armchairs, so I went for the other.

"Is it all right for us to talk in here?" I whispered, unsure of the club's rules.

"Yes. Honestly, I think more napping than reading happens in these rooms. You wouldn't believe the snoring."

I laughed at the image and folded my coat over the back of my chair. After sitting beside Jack, I crossed my gams at the knees and smoothed my kneeduster.

A middle-aged man with a tray entered the room and set out the coffee cups, sugar, and cream before leaving without a word. Once Williams was safely gone, Jack reached for his bag. He pulled out newspaper clippings and a few notes written in his own hand.

"I fear your missing high priest may be in more danger than you thought," he said, handing me the newspaper clippings.

My eyes widened as I read headlines about young witches whose bodies had been found. Some of them had pictures of the witches' corpses on the sides of roads or in ditches with their throats gaping like gruesome second mouths.

I shuddered at the images.

"The articles all describe the same scenario as Mr.

Nimzic's. They had all been acting strange, had a new lover who nobody seemed to know, and disappeared without a word," Jack informed. "The cases go back for over half a decade. When you told me about the circumstances around his disappearance, it reminded me of something I'd read a few years ago. This is what I dug up."

My stomach rolled, and I could not give voice to my horror. *Who could do such a thing?*

"The killer seems to target young, adult witches and murders them all in the same way: a slash to the throat. He kills them somewhere unknown then dumps the bodies. They're drained of blood, but there's none at the scenes. The press seemed to pick up on the similarities, but the police have never acknowledged the cases could be related."

"Is there anything else that connects the victims?"

"Not that I can see. They're all different races and are both male and female."

"I can understand why the coppers never picked up on it. With the crimes being so spread out, it's not likely to be a mass murderer."

Jack handed me a paper with a list of six names. "Here's the victim list. I couldn't find the names of the covens. If you can, maybe their fellow coven members can tell you more than what's printed in the newspaper. Let's hope the cases turn out to be unrelated to yours."

"Thanks, Jack. Did you find anything about Mr. Nimzic or his lover?"

He shook his head. "There doesn't seem to be a lot of information on Mr. Nimzic. The only records on him are basic. There wasn't even anything about him becoming the high priest of a large coven. Though if it was after prohibition, that would make sense. My source told me everyone seems to like him. He didn't say anything about a mysterious lover, but he did mention a singer at The Black Moon."

I nodded. "Rose. I met her yesterday. She didn't seem too upset Mr. Nimzic is missing, though she did say they're on the breaks. Still, it felt like she was hiding something. She and Jesse had an unusual conversation."

Jack's aquamarine eyes sharpened, telling me he'd noticed I'd referred to Jesse by his first name.

"Jesse Hunt? The man who hired you?"

"Yeah, I know I said for you to check on his relationship with Mr. Nimzic, but I think they're just friends as he says."

"I'm not so sure about that."

My heart skipped a beat. "What do you mean?"

He squinted, and I stilled.

"There are a few suspicious circumstances surrounding Mr. Hunt. It seems he's been close with a coven leader before, one who wound up dead."

I could feel the blood drain from my face, but I kept my voice steady. "You think Jesse murdered him?"

Jack frowned. "There's no evidence of that. He seems to have died of natural causes. However, when I asked my source about him, he was reluctant to spill. Eventually, he told me your client's parents had been murdered. It may be a coincidence. But in light of his best friend's disappearance, it's suspicious to say the least."

"His parents were murdered and a coven leader he was close with died? No wonder he's so desperate to find his friend even though the evidence showed he left voluntarily," I mused.

Jack squinted at my sympathy for Jesse and stood. "Don't you think hiring you could be a ruse to cover up his own involvement in Mr. Nimzic's disappearance?" he asked while pacing.

"Is there any evidence that links Jesse to the witch murders? Or proof that he had anything to do with the death of his parents or friend?" I ask defensively, rising to my feet.

Jack blinked, taken aback by my tone. "Not that I know of, but what do you really know about Jesse Hunt?"

I couldn't stop the thought: *I know his presence shakes me.* I shivered and mentally slapped myself. "I know he wants to find his friend. He's genuinely worried," I asserted with confidence.

Jack's frown tugged at my heart. I wasn't used to arguing with him, but I refused to back down. "You've found no evidence that Jesse Hunt is suspicious?" he asked doubtfully.

Benji's warning, Patrick's suspicions, and his mysterious exchange with Rose. I shook my head. *Nothing that overrides my gut reaction to him.*

Jack took a step closer to me and stared into my eyes. "You're not being honest, Anna."

I averted my gaze.

"Why're you so determined that Jesse is clean? You're usually logical and thorough in your investigations," Jack wondered.

"It's just my gut," I mumbled.

"Your gut has never been a good enough reason to ignore suspicious circumstances such as these."

I didn't respond because he was right. He moved in closer to me. His scent relaxed my building tension, and I looked up at him.

"What's really going on, Anna?" he asked, concerned. "Are you all right?"

I couldn't lie to Jack when he looked at me with such sincere trepidation. I avoided his gaze. "I don't know what's gotten into me. Jesse distracts me. When he's around, my body…reacts. I feel so guilty. It's like my body is betraying me, and I can't help but think of how much it would hurt Cy."

Looking up again, I saw Jack's face crumpled in pain. "You're too cruel," he whispered as if he couldn't take a full breath.

Alarm shot through me. I reached up to place my hand on Jack's arm, but he jerked out of my reach. "Don't," he quietly demanded.

My stomach dropped, and I felt like I was going to upchuck. "Jack…"

"I'm sorry. I'm not strong enough to do this again. I know I promised I'd be whatever you needed me to be, but I can't be your sanctuary in this situation."

Silent tears flowed down my face unhindered at Jack's sudden rejection.

He winced at my tears, but he didn't take it back.

I swallowed around the lump in my throat. "Why?" I managed to ask.

He looked astonished. "You don't know?"

I shook my head.

He sighed, discouraged, then met my eyes seriously. "Do you want to know?"

I nodded.

He stepped close to me again and lifted his hands to my cheeks, wiping my tears with his thumbs.

I met his eyes curiously, waiting for his reason.

He sealed my lips with his.

My heart hammered, and my entire body combusted. Having not been touched in nearly a decade, my desire made up for lost time as if to prove it still worked.

He kissed me like his life depended on it. The passion in his heart had broken the dam, and it all flowed into me.

I was drowning in it, and my head spun. The heat that spread through me didn't stop me from shivering.

Jack pulled back but kept his lips close to mine. "I love you, Anna," he whispered, his breath caressing my lips.

He kissed me feverishly again.

He continued to speak in between kisses, which burned me like the warmth of a fire heating frozen flesh.

"I've always loved you."

I barely registered what he was saying as I begged for more of what he happily gave.

"Since the day we met, I knew I'd never love anyone else."

A painful throbbing in my core screamed at him not to stop.

"I tried to respect your wishes when you chose him," he murmured.

I nudged toward him for more, but he held my face just out of reach as he continued to spill.

I whimpered in need. However, the urgency in his eyes made me listen quietly.

"I even tried to find love with others. You remember. Right?"

My mind spun, trying to comprehend his meaning. *Love with others? I remember Jack dating some women in college, but it never worked out. I don't care. Just kiss me again.*

I nodded to show I understood and pushed forward once more, but he wasn't finished talking.

"It only brought me pain. Every time I touched someone else, I thought only of you," he lamented.

His eyes pleaded with me, and I stomped on my desire in order to give him the attention he needed. "Anna, please don't put me through that again. Put me out of my misery."

I finally understood what he was asking. As he leaned in to kiss me again, it took all my strength to pull away.

His look of dejection ripped my heart out.

"I'm sorry," I choked. "Jack, you're the most important person to me, and the one person I can never be with."

"Say it clearly so I can repeat it to myself later," he murmured, defeated.

I didn't want to hurt him anymore, so I didn't speak.

"Tell me," he demanded flatly.

"You're the one person Cy would never want me to be with."

He nodded stiffly and moved toward the door. "I'm sorry, but I don't think I can give you a ride back to the city. I'll ask the doorman to call you a cab."

He left me alone with my body still craving his warmth and what was left of my heart limp on the floor.

SEVENTEEN

FJOLNIR

"You're saying you want to help? Are you sure?" I asked in feigned doubt. I rewarded Leo with a smile, as he nodded enthusiastically.

"Thank you. You're so talented. Your skills would be greatly appreciated," I flattered.

I was glad to see the spell was working so well that we didn't have to keep him tied up and asleep anymore. Since I had full-time access to him, his infatuation had become firmly rooted in his mind. As long as I kept dosing him, he'd stay that way until the end.

He followed me to the barn where Raven awaited us. They weren't surprised to see each other, but they didn't greet each other either.

"What do I need to do?" Leo asked eagerly.

I handed him a piece of paper and a ceremonial knife. "I need you to draw this magic circle with your blood."

He frowned a little at using blood magic.

"Don't worry. I'm going to help. It's all in preparation for our big night," I encouraged.

His eyes gleamed in excitement. "What're you going to do?" he asked.

"Raven and I have already drawn our parts of the circle, as you can see." I pointed at the circles and sigils on the floor surrounding the altar. "And we've been charging it a little every day."

Leo looked sharply at Raven, who grinned wickedly.

"But Leo, it's your part on the final night that's the most important," I distracted.

He beamed with pride.

"I've never heard of a spell like this. What's it for?" Leo frowned again, trying to think.

"This is going to make all my dreams come true. I thought you said you wanted to help," I demanded in a deeper tone.

"Of course I do, Fjolnir," he assured me.

"I knew I could count on you, Leo." I smiled and captured his chin.

His eyes glazed over as I kissed him deeply. Pulling him into an embrace, I whispered in his ear. "While you're drawing the circle, I want you to watch everything I do to Raven and imagine what I'm going to do to you." I licked his earlobe before pulling away.

Raven's eyes heated with jealousy at the exchange. *Good. The ritual will go even better if he has strong emotions while charging the circle.*

I nodded to Raven, and we went to the altar.

Smiling over my shoulder at Leo, I said, "You can start any time."

He stared at the paper I'd given him then cut his hand with the knife, making a little puddle of blood in his cupped palm to draw with.

I turned my attention back to Raven, who sat on the altar impatiently. I spread his knees and stood between his legs. His black eyes sparkled with anticipation. Bringing my lips gently down to his, I smiled as he gasped in desire.

"I like that expression," I teased him, running my hand down his arm and under his shirt.

I traced his chest and stomach, and he panted in between kisses.

He unbuttoned my shirt as I stroked and grasped his thighs. I allowed him to brush his lips to my collarbone and chest. Like always, I remained limp until he reached down and cupped me. The stimulation didn't fail, and Raven smiled as I stiffened in his hand.

I looked over at Leo, who watched us on all fours, trembling with parted lips as he painted with his blood. I smiled suggestively at him, and he flushed with yearning.

Demanding attention, Raven unbuttoned my pants, and they fell to the floor. He knelt before me reverently and took my cock deep into his mouth. Warmth spread through me, and my balls tightened as my desire rose. I shivered and moaned as he thoroughly licked my shaft. He murmured softly with gratification between wet sucking sounds.

Before I could lose my momentum, I pulled away from his mouth and quickly removed his pants. He turned around and braced his hands on the altar. I pressed my chest to his back, kissing and biting the nape of his neck. Reaching around, I palmed his ready cock and stroked him slowly. He ground his ass against my still-slippery tip.

Gripping his hips with both hands, I slid into him, and we voiced our mutual pleasure.

I let Raven handle directing the energy released into the circle as I worked us both to completion, my necklace striking my chest with every thrust.

EIGHTEEN

ANNA

I didn't see Jack as I trudged to the lobby. Though the doorman told me it would be a few minutes before the taxi arrived, I waited outside in the cold. The numbness that crept into my limbs was just a physical manifestation of how dead I felt inside.

I've been hurting the kindest and most deserving man in the world for the majority of my life. Jack has loved and supported me, and I can't give him the one thing he's ever asked me for. He'd take me knowing how broken I am, and I won't even take a small step toward him.

My depression turned to anger. *You're tormenting Jack because of something Cy said before he broke up with you? Cy is dead, and he's probably broken your soulmate bond anyway.*

When the dimbox arrived, the doorman beckoned to the driver as I was climbing in. The cabbie got out and approached him. They had a short conversation, and the driver returned to the cab. I told him to take me to my office.

As my limbs began to thaw in the relative warmth of the motorcar, my body remembered the heat of Jack's touch. I squirmed uncomfortably.

Why can't you just love Jack? He's one of the reasons you're still alive and functional today. You wouldn't have gone to see Lillian and found a sustainable equilibrium if it wasn't for the fact that you didn't want to hurt him. Jack could make you happy again.

I imagined Jack's smiling face and the warmth of his arms around me.

I don't deserve to be happy, especially not with Jack. I hurt Cy so badly that he couldn't stand the thought of being with me. I'd probably end up hurting Jack worse than I already have. He's better off without me. I still have Dad and Aunt Vi, and I can't let the time Dad has left be marred by my depression.

I reached into my bag to pay the cabbie, and I felt the newspaper clippings Jack had given me. I scowled at myself. *Here I am feeling sorry for myself when Leo could be in serious danger. I may be heartless, but I'm not useless. If I can help others, that's enough for me for now.*

I held out the greens to the driver, but he shook his head and waved my hand away. "That fancy man in the red coat already paid the fare," he explained.

"The doorman?" I asked.

The cabbie nodded.

Jack... My chest tightened. *Even after I hurt you, you're still taking care of me.* Before my tears could spill over, I shook myself and got out of the dimbox.

I still had time before I could see Elizabeth Shelton, so I went to the diner. I ordered a bowl of soup, knowing my stomach couldn't handle much else at the moment.

As I sipped my liquid meal, I carefully read the clippings.

Six missing witches were later found dead: four women and two men, all in their early to mid-twenties. The first woman went missing seven years ago, and the others disappeared in annual increments. All of this happened in the area.

Jesse said he'd arrived only a year ago, and Lillian corroborated that story.

I still can't believe that Jesse's involved in the witch murders. However, Jack's right about my gut not usually being enough in suspicious circumstances. I need to find out more about Jesse Hunt, even if it's just to clear his name. I also need to talk to the victims' covens. Benji should be getting back to me soon. I'll ask him what he knows.

I felt warm after sitting in the diner and eating hot soup. The feeling reminded me of Jack again. It seemed my body refused to forget its unleashed desire.

To get rid of it, I decided to walk to Elizabeth Shelton's. It wasn't too far, but it was far enough that I'd normally have taken a streetcar.

The Shelton's home was a row house like Leo's, but the street seemed livelier due to its proximity to a busy road. As I mounted the three narrow steps, I could hear loud music playing inside. I rang the bell twice, hoping the occupants could hear it.

A frazzled-looking woman with graying, black hair answered with a tired smile. "Yes? How can I help you?" she asked.

"Hello, my name is Anna Caill. I'm here to see Miss Elizabeth Shelton."

The woman looked worried. "Are you from her school?"

A teenage girl with short black hair and a lean build came running to the door. "For crying out loud, Mom. She's not from school. She's the private detective who's looking for Leo. Patrick told me she was coming."

Mrs. Shelton frowned. "Well, you should have told me, Elizabeth."

"But she's here to see me not you."

Mrs. Shelton smiled at me again. "I'm sorry. I wasn't aware you were coming. Please come in."

I returned her smile and thanked her for her hospitality.

"We can talk in here." Elizabeth waved me into a sitting room where a Victrola blasted upbeat jazz.

"Elizabeth, lower the volume," Mrs. Shelton censured.

"Rhatz, this is the best part, too." Elizabeth shut the Victrola's doors and flopped onto the couch, tucking her legs under her.

I smiled at her. "I like this song, too," I said.

"And how! It's the cat's whiskers," Elizabeth gushed.

"Elizabeth! That is not how ladies speak or sit," Mrs. Shelton scolded, swatting Elizabeth's leg.

Elizabeth rolled her eyes.

"Mrs. Shelton, could I trouble you for a cup of tea?" I asked, trying to occupy the wrinkle.

"Of course, please make yourself comfortable," Mrs. Shelton said as she left the room.

I sat across from Elizabeth. "Miss Shelton, you said Mr. Sullivan informed you I would be visiting?"

"Call me Lizzie. Yeah, Patrick called me yesterday. He said you'd be coming and told me to answer all your questions."

"When did you find out about Mr. Nimzic's disappearance?"

"Patrick called me the day after Leo told me he was going to officially name me his successor at the next full moon gathering. Patrick wanted to know if Leo had shown for our meeting and if he'd said anything about where he was going next. I told him Leo had met with me, and he'd said he was going home but was planning on meeting Jesse later."

"You're aware that Mr. Nimzic didn't meet Mr. Hunt as planned?"

She nodded.

"Did Mr. Nimzic say anything about meeting anyone else before Mr. Hunt?"

She shook her head. "No, but he did say he was expecting a telephone call."

"Do you know who he was expecting a call from?"

She looked to the door then waved me toward her. I got up and sat next to her on the couch.

"Leo had been seeing someone recently. He didn't want me to say anything, but he was expecting a call from him," she whispered.

"Mr. Nimzic told you about his male lover?" I asked quietly.

She nodded. "A while ago, Leo received a letter asking for help. It's normal for coven leaders to get notes like that. He showed it to me as an example of the type of requests high priests get. The fella who wrote the letter said he'd joined one of those witch rehabilitation groups churches sponsor to stop witches from using magic."

I dipped my head to show I knew what she meant.

"It seems this man was having second thoughts, and he'd heard Leo was an approachable coven leader. He asked if Leo would meet to talk to him. Well, of course, Leo wasn't going to refuse to help someone."

"Did it say where they were to meet?"

"It just said the bar above The Shadow Market."

"Where's that?"

She frowned. "I don't know. Leo wouldn't tell me, but he seemed nervous about the location."

"Did he go?"

She nodded. "He went, and that's when Leo started

acting fluky. I asked him what was bothering him. At first, he said he just had some feelings to work out. But eventually, he told me he was going to break up with Rose because he'd developed feelings for the fella who wrote the letter."

"Was the letter signed?"

"No, but it said he'd be waiting for Leo at a certain day and time. It told him to look for a man with blond hair wearing a red scarf."

Mrs. Shelton entered with a tea tray and poured me a cup, which I didn't drink. I was grateful the saucer kept the too pleasant warmth from my hands.

"Is there anything else you can think of that may help?" I asked Lizzie.

She shook her head.

"What about Mr. Hunt? What do you know about him?"

Her brows furrowed in confusion. "Jesse? Not much. We aren't around each other except for official coven functions. He and Leo are good friends. They met about a year ago, and Jesse joined the coven not long after."

"What about the seal in Mr. Nimzic's house? Mr. Hunt said it had been broken. Do you know anything about that?"

Lizzie and Mrs. Shelton mirrored each other's looks of surprise.

Lizzie shook her head again as Mrs. Shelton expressed alarm. "His seal was broken? How frightening! What about the seal on his sanctum?"

"As far as I know, it's still intact."

They both sighed in relief.

"Thank you for your cooperation. Please let me know if you think of anything else." I put my untouched tea on the table and handed Lizzie my card.

"I hope you find him soon," Lizzie said.

"Don't worry. I'll find him," I reassured.

I thanked Mrs. Shelton for the tea as she showed me out.

NINETEEN

After walking to the main street, I didn't have to wait long for the streetcar, and I only had to transfer once to get to Jesse's apartment building.

Jesse blinked when he opened the door to find me, and he stared uncomprehendingly for a moment. He looked enticing, and I let out a low breath in appreciation. His golden-brown hair was tousled as if he'd been lying down while reading. The top two buttons of his shirt were undone, and he held a snifter in his hand.

I gritted my teeth and steeled my nerves. "Can I come in?" I asked.

"Yeah, sorry," he said, stepping aside. "I was expecting you to call by telephone," he explained.

"I have a lot to talk about. It was easier this way." I hung up my coat and hat.

"It's no problem. Would you like a drink?"

I looked at the glass in his hand. *Bourbon sounds good, but I don't want to feel warm right now.* "No, thanks."

He nodded, and we both sat on the divan.

"I met Lizzie. It seems she knew about Mr. Nimzic's

male lover. She didn't know his name or how to reach him, though. Apparently, this fella wrote to Mr. Nimzic asking for help. She also said he was blond like his neighbor did, which reminds me. Have you found out what that charm bag under his bed is?"

"I haven't. I'm still looking into it. So Leo saw Lizzie earlier the day he was supposed to meet me. Did she say why he'd gone to see her?"

I paused. *I'm not sure I want to tell Jesse that Leo was naming Lizzie his successor. That seems like coven business and not my place to talk about. Also, it doesn't feel pertinent to the investigation.* "She didn't say. But you said he told you he was going to meet someone earlier in the day. That must've been Lizzie. According to her, he was only waiting for a telephone call before he was going to meet you."

Jesse stared at me as if he could see I was lying, but he didn't call me on it. "It sounds like we're running into a lot of dead ends."

"It is discouraging, but I still have a few irons in the fire."

I watched him sip his whiskey in thought. Then, he looked at me expectantly, waiting for me to continue. When I didn't say anything, he met my eyes knowingly.

"You heard something about me. Didn't you?"

I averted my gaze.

"That bad, eh?"

He leaned toward me and smiled encouragingly.

"You can ask me. I've got nothing to hide."

"I heard about your parents," I answered quietly.

He smirked. "I guess no one is fast enough to outrun rumors. You want to hear my story? Of course you do. I must look awfully suspicious to a private detective."

I could hear the bitterness in his voice, and I opened my mouth to say he didn't have to tell me.

"I don't mind telling you." He met my eyes earnestly. "I have a feeling we're similar. We've both experienced pain and loss, and we've both had to find a way to carry on. People like us have a look about us."

My heart fluttered at being seen through.

"How should I start?" he mused, leaning back.

"I'm sure you know witches' magic comes from the fact our souls are different from human souls. In order to ensure witch souls are born into witch families, there's a ritual parents perform to attract a witch's soul to a fetus during pregnancy. Of course, there are witches who end up being born into human families. I'm one such as this. Before witches came out of the shadows, we had a hard time finding human-born witches. But when we lived openly, like when I was born, there were programs for such children.

"It was apparent from an early age that I was a witch. Since both my parents were human, my father was convinced I wasn't his. He took his suspicions out on my mother and me, and I got used to being called bastard more than my name.

"With no one to teach me, my magic was out of control. When I was scared or angry, things would break, fly across the room, or even burst into flame.

"I was around eight when Martin came to our house. He explained to my parents about me being a witch and invited me to join his coven. He said they'd give me lessons and teach me how to control my magic.

"My father told them to take me, though they were only supposed to be after school lessons. Martin saw my situation and agreed to take me in, but I didn't want to leave my mother alone with my father. I refused, and Martin said he'd return when I'd had time to think it over.

"That night, while my mother was tucking me into

bed, she tried to convince me to go with Martin. My father came stomping up the stairs to my room, demanding I pack my things.

"My mother went out, and I heard them arguing. She told him I was sleeping. He said he didn't care and to wake me anyway. I crawled out of bed and peeked through the crack in my door.

"As my father moved toward my room, my mother tried to block his way. He grabbed her by the throat and threw her down the stairs. I ran to help her, but it was too late.

"I screamed in fury and ended up burning the house down with my father still inside."

I sat, speechless, with my heart aching for his pain.

"What they say is true. I murdered my father."

When my words failed me, I gently grabbed his hand. He smiled with no joy and continued.

"Martin came back and took me in just like he'd promised. He even named me his successor, to the dismay of the other coven members. Unfortunately, he died before the ceremony could take place. Our coven's artifacts were lost, and the coven was disbanded."

I looked down at our hands and stroked his with my thumb. "You've been through a lot," I sympathized.

"You have, too. Haven't you?"

I met his eyes.

"You don't have to tell me. Sometimes not saying it aloud is the only way to deal with it."

I nodded.

He leaned in until our heads were close together. "You don't have to pretend with me. I know how exhausting it is to pretend all the time. You can wallow or writhe in the pain. It's all part of who you are, and it has its own dark beauty."

My heart pounded as his voice echoed in the depths of my soul. He inched closer until I felt his breath on my face.

"Will you show it to me?" he whispered. "I bet your soul hasn't been laid bare for a long time."

My body's reaction to Jesse, which I'd been trying to smother since our first meeting, coupled with the need Jack had unleashed snapped my self-control.

I kissed Jesse with urgency, and he didn't hold back.

Neither of us had any desire to go slow. He pushed my skirt up and pulled me onto his lap. As he grasped my thighs, he paused only for a second when his hand found the knife I always kept sheathed in my garter. Rather than making him stop, it seemed to excite him more.

I could already feel his stiff cock hard against my core as I leaned back and he kissed my neck. I clutched his hips with my knees, and he grabbed my ass. Supporting my weight, he lifted me as he stood. I wrapped my legs around his waist as he carried me to the bedroom while smothering me in kisses.

Opening the door, he broke our kiss and spoke words of magic. A crowd of candles lit up the room. He dropped us both onto the bed, and I started tugging at his clothes.

I was getting nowhere, so he stood and removed them himself. I quickly discarded my own with the frustration of impatience. His husky voice advised me to leave my garter with the knife on.

We took a short moment to appreciate the sight of each other in the candlelight.

I reached for Jesse, and he obliged.

As he pressed my body with his solid weight, he whispered in my ear, "Scream out your pain. I want to make your dark soul dance."

"Yes," I breathed.

We both shuddered and moaned as he thrust into my core. I lifted my hips, and he went deeper with every drive.

I wasn't quiet as I shouted my approval, and he smiled in agreement. Everything I'd been holding in—all the sadness, all the agony, all the frustration, all the loneliness, and all the despair—I bared it all to Jesse, and his eyes said it was beautiful.

As we stretched the dark wings of our souls and flew through the pain and pleasure, I didn't think of Cy or Jack even once.

TWENTY

"Say it clearly so I can repeat it to myself later," he said, defeated.

I didn't respond.

"Tell me," he demanded flatly.

"You're the one person Cy would never want me to be with."

I awoke with a flinch after reliving the memory from the day before. I could still feel Jack's lips burning mine as I lay in Jesse's arms.

I felt the same sorrow and self-loathing I had right after I'd rejected Jack. I pushed it away and thought about the situation I was in. I'd expected to feel ashamed for being with someone other than Cy, but I couldn't seem to surface from my body's fulfillment.

I observed my new comfort with fascination. It felt like when I accidentally cut myself. The injury hurts, but after the initial pain, I watch my blood drip down my finger. It stung to think about Cy, but there was also a sense of dark satisfaction. However, as my mind touched on Jack, I drew back like I'd been burned. The pain of that encounter still seemed too fresh.

While most of the candles in Jesse's room had burned out, the few that remained illuminated the furniture, casting long shadows. Other than the bed and nightstand, there was a bookshelf and a small altar in the corner.

When my gaze fell on Jesse, who was looking down at me as he held me to his chest, his warm brown eyes were gentle. *Jesse saw me for who I am. Not only did he accept me, but he told me I wasn't broken and showed me that even my darkest depths are beautiful.*

"Did you have a bad dream?" he asked in a raspy voice.

"Something like that."

I took stock of my body and discovered the ever-present anxiety, which seemed so much a part of my everyday life, was gone. In its place was a heavy satiated feeling, similar to what I felt like after Living Memory but more so. It was the difference between not being hungry and being full. It was the difference between living in my past and my present.

Looking at Jesse, the seed of hope was sown in the tear-soaked soil of my soul. "What time is it?" I asked.

"It's still early. The sun isn't up yet."

Our naked bodies were intertwined under the blankets. Readjusting my position, I felt the taut muscles of Jesse's abdomen under my fingertips. His hips twitched, and I met his eyes with a question. *No more thinking for now. I need to live in the moment.* His answer was to pull my lips to his.

There was no hurry in our deepening kiss. It was as

slow and careful as the night before had been reckless and urgent.

As Jesse thoroughly kissed me, I stroked his chest and stomach. The combination heated his blood, and he rolled me onto my back.

He ran his lips and tongue over my neck and collarbone, and my breath hitched. His fingertips gently stroked the lines of my body from my shoulder to my thighs and back. I shivered as need bubbled inside me like molten metal in a crucible.

I reached for his stiff cock as it pressed against my thigh, but he gently pinned my wrists above my head. I took the hint and kept them there as he trailed down my arms and rubbed my nipples with his thumbs.

I hummed a groan and squirmed beneath him. Smiling, he dipped his head to my breast and took my tight nipple into his mouth. I hissed as he flicked it with his tongue.

Just as I was reaching my limit, he flipped me onto my stomach and pulled my hips until they were propped up and my front rested on my elbows.

I gasped as he stuck his tongue deep into my core and lapped at me. He grabbed my hips and rocked them back and forth, licking me hard with a wide tongue.

I had a difficult time supporting my weight as I shuddered and screamed.

My core was swollen, wet, and throbbing after he'd worked it. I pulled him onto the bed and pinned him under me.

As I straddled him, I smiled with confidence, and his eyes were glazed with lust. I pushed his blunt tip to the brink of my core and took him in all at once. It was foreign and uncomfortable at first, but eventually, he filled me up in a way that made me feel empty without him inside me.

His hips jacked as he grunted. I rocked slowly, resting my palms on his stomach when he tried to speed up. When it was clear he couldn't take it anymore, I let him pick the pace. He grasped my thighs and drove us both to our peaks.

Feeling like gluttons, we floated in the afterglow for a while before he spoke.

"I can't wait for you to meet Leo. He's truly magnanimous. He knows about my past but still treats me with the same kindness and generosity he does everyone else. If only everyone was like him."

"I'm sorry you aren't surrounded by such understanding people."

He chuckled. "You're talking about Patrick. Aren't you? It's true. We don't really get along, but I appreciate his efforts to look out for Leo."

"Still, he seemed harsh. He suggested you may have had something to do with Mr. Nimzic's disappearance. He even thought you'd cloaked his location to prevent someone from finding him with magic."

Jesse hummed a question. "Did he? I'm sure he must've had a reason for his suspicions, though."

I propped myself up on my elbow and looked down at Jesse. "I don't know if I should be the one to tell you this, but Patrick thinks you were lying about meeting Mr. Nimzic that night. He was coming to see you to tell you he was choosing Lizzie as his successor."

Jesse didn't react for a while. Finally, he said, "That explains a lot. If Leo was coming to deliver unpleasant news, it makes sense that people would think a murderer like me would react violently. But I don't really want to be the coven's next high priest. I only agreed to consider it because Leo asked me as a favor. I'd already been trained by Martin, and Leo wasn't sure if Lizzie was ready yet."

I sighed in relief at his logical explanation. I hadn't realized how much I was suspecting him until my suspicions were gone.

"I wasn't going to tell you this because I didn't want to alarm you unnecessarily. However, you may know something that could help. Over the last seven years, a number of witches have gone missing in the area. Six of them have been found murdered. Have you heard anything about it?"

"No," Jesse said warily.

"The cases could be unrelated, but it seems like the circumstances surrounding their disappearances were similar to Mr. Nimzic's. I'm planning on talking to some of their coven members to see if there are any related clues. If I show you the list of victims, could you tell me which covens they belong to?"

"If I recognize the names, I can." Jesse seemed understandably worried about this development.

"It could have nothing to do with Mr. Nimzic." I tried to reassure him again while censuring myself for telling him at all. *Still, if he knows which covens they came from, it'll be worth it.*

As daylight seeped through the edges of Jesse's bedroom curtains, I thought about how this solution may be better than Living Memory. My body felt too warm and my mind too hazy to be distracted by thoughts of the past. Considering what she'd told me the day before, I knew Lillian would be pleased with my conclusion.

Instead of going to Lillian's, I decided to indulge my desire one last time before going to work.

I smiled at Jesse, and he watched me curiously. I pulled the covers over my head and kissed down his torso. Before I could reach my destination, Jesse stopped me.

"I'm going to wash up. Why don't you start the coffee, and then you can use the shower?"

I tried to stifle my feeling of rejection as I lay naked and lonely in bed. *He's right. We don't have time for this. Leo could be in danger.*

TWENTY-ONE

When I emerged from the shower, Jesse handed me a plate with eggs on toast. I ate quickly and thanked him for the meal. Passing him the victim list from my bag, I asked if he recognized anyone.

He stared intently then shook his head. "What's your next move?" he asked, sipping his cup of joe.

"If I don't hear from my contact today, I'll go see Lillian."

"That's a good idea. She knows a lot of witches. What would you like me to do?"

"Wait here until I call you. I hope to have a direction by tonight."

He frowned but nodded.

Jesse followed me to the door and watched as I put on my hat and coat. "I'll see you later." I smiled easily.

"I'll be here," he stated.

After shutting the door behind me, I descended the stairs and shivered in the late morning air. The steel gray clouds hung low as if threatening those below.

I took the streetcar to my office. Maggie sat at her desk, smiling as she hung up the telephone.

"Who was that?" I asked, taking off my coat and hat.

"Benji," she answered, winking at the telephone as if he could see her.

"What did he say?"

"He said to tell you the coffee at Jake's isn't bad if you get there at noon when they grind freshly roasted beans."

I looked at the clock. It was 11:30.

"Is that all he said?"

She grinned. "All I have time to tell you."

Maybe I'm finally catching a break. "Did anyone else call?" I asked as I headed toward my office to change my clothes.

"Yeah, Detective Hartley. He said he came up empty, but he asked me to encourage you to come to dinner."

I shook my head as I entered my office. I changed quickly and returned, putting my coat and hat back on. "Call my dad. Won't you?"

She agreed as I reached for the door.

Jake's was a café not far from the cemetery entrance to Starlight Avenue. Contrary to Benji's comment, they had excellent coffee.

I sat in the far back corner of the café and ordered their specialty.

Benji approached just as the waiter brought my order. He made a show of looking me up and down. The waiter stiffened, preparing to come to my defense.

"May I join you?" Benji asked as though we'd never met.

I decided to play along and smiled like I was interested. "Grab a flop, baby," I simpered in my best impression of Rose's voice.

He took a seat beside me and ordered the same as I had. The waiter went away thinking we'd just met. We continued to smile and make eyes at each other until his coffee arrived and we were alone.

Benji chuckled, and I rolled my eyes.

"I almost believed you." He grinned.

"Banana oil. What've you got for me?"

Benji pursed his lips, but he leaned closer and lowered his voice. "I think the place you're looking for is called Erostes."

"Is it above The Shadow Market?"

Benji frowned. "How did you know?"

"I just found out yesterday that the bar above The Shadow Market is where Mr. Nimzic first met his lover."

He pouted.

"But I didn't know the name of it, so thanks, Benji. Can you tell me where it is?"

"You'll have to go in the topside entrance. Not just anyone can get into The Shadow Market. It's more protected than any other part of Starlight Avenue. I can't even get in."

"Okay."

"It's on 14th Place near Wimbly Avenue."

"How do I get in?"

"You have to bring an offering and pray to one of the Erostes."

"That's it?"

He met my eyes seriously. "Don't take it so lightly. You never know what could happen when you call on the ancient gods."

"Even as a human?"

"The gods may have preferred groups, but they watch over us all."

A little shaken by Benji's sudden, solemn demeanor, I pulled out the victim list and handed it to him.

"Can you tell me which covens these witches belonged to?"

He stared at the paper. "Are you also investigating the Phantom?"

I tilted my head in a question.

"That's what we call the killer who's been abducting witches and slitting their throats."

"So you recognize the names?"

He nodded. "But I only know of two of them. Charlie Miller was a member of Romesti, and Catherine Kelly was in Elroca. Their families both run businesses on Starlight Avenue. Ask for Miller's Magical Tools and The Emerald Herbalist."

Thanking him, I took the list back.

Benji watched me with concern. "You need to be careful if you're looking into the Phantom."

"I will," I assured him.

As I stood to mooch, Benji whispered, "You're staying clear of Hunt. Right?"

I covered my guilt with a smile. "Don't worry so much. You'll give yourself wrinkles and ruin that pretty face."

"I knew you thought I was pretty," he called to me while I made my escape.

TWENTY-TWO

B ack at Jesse's, I told him what I'd learned.

"I think going to Erostes first is a better choice. We know Mr. Nimzic and his lover were there, and the bartender or waiters might know something."

Jesse nodded and got ready to blouse.

"Wait." I stopped him at the door. "What sort of offerings do gods like?"

We went to a florist on the way as Jesse said flowers made nifty offerings. I held the bouquets in my lap while he drove us to Erostes.

The rose petals were so soft; I couldn't resist the urge to press my lips to them. *Roses are the perfect symbol of love. They're soft and smell intoxicating but can hurt you with their thorns. They're happiest when they grow wild and unhindered. And when someone tries to possess them by cutting them and putting them in a vase, they quickly wither and die.*

I looked over at Jesse. *My seed of hope could be a rosebush. My time with him has been wild and unhindered. I need to try not to hold on too tight.*

Unbidden, Jack's voice rang in my head. *"I even tried to*

find love with others." The feeling of his breath on my mouth made me flush. I cranked the window down so cold air could blow on my face.

"Are you warm?" Jesse asked, no doubt finding it unusual that I opened the window in winter.

"I just need some fresh air."

Erostes looked like a stone abbey. It seemed the perfect place to commune with the gods and to act as an entrance to The Shadow Market, but it didn't look much like a bar.

The brick walkway leading to the modest entrance was even and well cared for. The trees, which twisted in the small lawn, looked dried and naked as if dead rather than slumbering.

"This is a bar?" I asked Jesse doubtfully as he pulled on the thick iron ring to open the door.

"Think of it more like a hotel or retreat. Hotels have bars in them. Don't they?"

"You've been here?" I asked incredulously.

"It isn't only for homosexuals. It's more a place that welcomes everyone."

We entered a long, dark hallway. Every ten feet or so, there was a recessed area on one wall or the other where a statue stood on a raised platform. Beneath each statue burned candles and incense. Fruit was artfully piled on plates, and flowers overflowed in vases, their petals falling into bowls of creamy milk and glistening honey.

Before stepping farther in, Jesse stopped at a waist-high marble pillar with a bowl carved into the top. He rinsed his face and hands in the water collected in the bowl, and I repeated his actions. My hands ached with chill when I submerged them in the freezing, clear water.

"Choose who you want to make an offering to," Jesse instructed.

I didn't know any of these gods or goddesses, but I

looked at the statues carefully. One at the end seemed to call to me, so I placed the roses at his feet. His virile, manly form stood naked, and his proud wings flanked him. The name etched into the platform that supported him read, "Eros."

"Hello, Eros, I'm Anna Caill," I started awkwardly in a low voice. I looked over my shoulder self-consciously and saw Jesse standing before a goddess farther down the hall. "I don't know what you're the god of, but I hope you accept this offering and bless me."

The longer I stared at the expertly sculpted marble, the more I felt like it would be warm to the touch.

Jesse moved toward me and stood quietly by, waiting for me to finish.

I tore my eyes away from Eros and hoofed to the end of the hall, where an unguarded door waited.

"What happens if you don't bring an offering?" I asked curiously.

"Then, the door won't open."

Behind the door was a courtyard with a fountain in the middle and doors or paths leading away on all sides. The fountain was empty of water, and the courtyard was deserted. *I imagine this place is much livelier in the summer.* A girl with her arms full of folded towels bustled from one hallway to another without acknowledging us.

I followed Jesse through a set of double doors at the other end of the courtyard. We entered a chic bar full of cozy tables, some of which looked strategically placed in dark corners. The bar was somewhere in between busy and uninhabited. A smooth-looking youth played dulcet tones on a piano at the far end.

We sat at the bar and waited for the bartender to notice us. I ordered a Bourbon neat, and Jesse asked for a scotch on the rocks.

As Jesse handed him the chips, I leaned in to grab his attention. "Have you seen a man with blond hair and a red scarf come in here?" I asked him.

He eyed me suspiciously. "What's it to you?"

"The fella stole something dear to me, and I just want it back is all."

"This thing valuable?" the bartender asked with piqued interest.

"Not to anyone but me. But if it's berries you're after, I can make it worth your while."

The bartender raised one eyebrow and tapped the bar. I slipped a five onto the polished wood, and he set a glass on top of it.

"I've seen a fella like that a few times. He usually walks on through if you know what I mean."

Walks through to The Shadow Market?

"Have you ever seen him meet a male witch in his twenties with black hair?" Jesse asked.

The bartender's eyes flicked to Jesse then back to me, and I nodded.

"Yeah, seems like I've seen them quite a bit these past few weeks."

"Do you know where we can find either of them?" I asked.

The bartender tilted his head toward a curtain that I would've guessed led to a storeroom.

"He went down not too long ago. Maybe he'll leave this way." The bartender took his payoff and went to help someone else.

"He could be at The Shadow Market right now," I murmured.

"Or he could've left through Starlight Avenue," Jesse countered.

"My informant said it's difficult to get access to the market."

Jesse thought for a while then said, "I might know a way in. But if it doesn't work, we'd both be in serious trouble."

I silently weighed our options. "What do you think?" I asked.

"I've heard the market is big. Even if we get in, we could miss him. I think I should go, and you should guard this door in case he slips past me."

I met his eyes worriedly. "Is it really that dangerous?"

"It'll be easier alone."

"All right," I agreed. "See if you can find him. I'll watch the door."

He nodded and walked through the curtained doorway without looking back.

TWENTY-THREE

FJOLNIR

Climbing the stone steps of The Shadow Market toward Erostes, I clutched the jar of salve in my coat pocket. *Leo's going through the stuff at a much quicker rate than I'd expected. I practically have to kiss him every hour.*

I pulled out my watch and looked at the time. *I better get back soon. The sleeping draught will be wearing off, and I don't want to leave them alone together for too long.*

The guard at the storeroom door nodded to me as I went through.

Leslie, the bartender, was in the storeroom looking for something. When he saw me, his eyes widened, and he motioned me closer.

"There's a pair asking after you at the bar. They didn't know much, but they asked about a blond man with a red scarf. They even mentioned that fella you've been seeing."

My pulse quickened. "Show me."

He pulled me close to the curtain, and I peeked through.

"See the flapper with the chestnut hair sitting at the bar?"

My heart pounded in my chest. *She's so beautiful.* My cock stiffened as I pictured my hands on her creamy skin.

"The fella with her went to The Shadow Market looking for you. He could be back any time." Leslie pulled me from my fantasy.

My lip twitched in distaste. *An invisibility spell would take too much magic.* I unwound the scarf from my neck and stuffed it into my pocket. Fabricating a glamour was fairly simple, especially when it only had to be held for a few minutes to fool a human. I made myself appear to her as someone with long, brown hair and a full beard. I pulled my hat down and my collar up. *If I go quickly, I should be fine.*

I took a deep breath and stepped out with confidence, walking with purpose. She looked up, and our eyes met. I held my breath. Squinting a little, she analyzed me with a calculating gaze.

I nodded to her, as that's what's polite when people make eye contact, and kept walking.

She tilted her head at me and went back to staring into her drink.

Keeping my pace steady, I left Erostes without further incident.

TWENTY-FOUR

ANNA

I t was twenty minutes after Jesse left before the curtain showed any movement. The bartender went back there in search of more olives. A few minutes later, a man emerged.

He had long, brown hair and a mountain man beard. His collar was pulled up, and his hat was pulled low. I accidentally met his eyes, and I squinted to try to see what color they were in the dim light.

He nodded to me politely, and I realized I was staring quite rudely. I inclined my head at him and gazed into my untouched drink.

In the hours that followed, a number of men and women came out of the curtained door. None of them matched the description of Leo's lover. Finally, Jesse returned, scowling. I shook my head at his unspoken question.

"I couldn't find him. He must've slipped past into Starlight Avenue," he sighed.

I chewed my lip in frustration. Thinking about what to do next, I said, "If Mr. Nimzic wasn't with him, maybe he's already home."

I followed Jesse to a telephone booth near the entrance of the bar. He tapped the side of the telephone box impatiently as he waited for the operator to connect him. After hanging up the earpiece, he came out and shook his head.

"Maybe his lover was just running an errand," I suggested.

"At The Shadow Market?" Jesse doubted.

"Well, I've heard they sell all manner of goods there. It's not all bad. Right? Some of it is just rare."

"That's true."

"Tomorrow, I'm going to visit the victims' families. At least then we can find out more about whether the cases are connected. If I really come up empty, we can come here every day until they show up, or we can go to The Shadow Market and ask around. Maybe someone there knows more than the bartender."

Jesse nodded. "Does that mean we're finished for the night?"

I bobbed my head and moved closer to him. Meeting his eyes, I touched his hand lightly. He put his hand in his coat pocket, but his gaze wasn't harsh. A blink later and his look of regret turned cool and distant.

"It sounds like you have a busy day tomorrow. You should get some rest. Would you like me to drop you off somewhere?"

He's right, but I still can't shake the feeling I was just given the icy mitt. "Please drop me at home," I said, trying to keep my voice from sounding too cold.

We didn't speak the entire way to my house, and the silence was suffocating. I knew something was off but the cause eluded me.

"Thanks for the ride. I'll contact you when I know more," I said before getting out of the motorcar.

He drove off while I was still on the curb.

It was late, so I wasn't surprised when the house was dark. I tried to be as quiet as possible when I entered, taking my shoes off at the door and keeping the lights out. As I tiptoed toward the stairs, a light flicked on above me. Aunt Vi stood at the top landing with her arms crossed, wearing a look of disapproval.

I froze and grimaced, raising my hand in greeting.

She silently descended and motioned for me to follow her to the kitchen.

I sat at the table, hanging my head and waiting for the lecture. Instead, Aunt Vi gave me a turkey sandwich and a glass of milk. I nodded my thanks and devoured the meal.

Watching me eat, Aunt Vi sighed. "You've had a difficult life already, and you're still so young. Your mother, your childhood friend, and with your father being sick... I'm scared for you, Anna. The world is an unforgiving place, especially for a woman."

She reached out and stroked my hair. "I know you've been hurting. But if you continue down this reckless path, I fear you'll never see the parts of life that are worth living for."

I've always thought of Aunt Vi as someone who's too hung up on appearances and what's "proper." I know she loves me, but I didn't know she had all of these fears locked away in her heart.

I stood and hugged her, resting my head on her shoulder as she patted it. "Don't worry, Aunt Vi. I may appear reckless, but I'm good at what I do. I've got no plans of leaving this life anytime soon."

I pulled back and gave her a cocky smile. "Besides, you know how stubborn I am. Can you see me giving up? Then who'd be here to cause you trouble?"

She chuckled and shook her head at me. "You're incorrigible."

"I'll take that as a compliment."

Clearing my dishes from the table, she shooed me.

"Goodnight," I said, kissing her on the cheek.

"Off to bed now," she dismissed.

I mounted the stairs as quietly as I could and slipped into my room. While I didn't mind sleeping on the couch in my office, there was nothing quite as comforting as my own bed. I changed into bedclothes and climbed into the cool sheets.

Drifting to sleep, I had no fear of Living Memory side effects.

I lay on a soft bed alone in the darkness. Straining my ears, I listened for any whisper of a sound. No matter how hard I tried, I could hear only my own breathing and the beating of my heart.

Finally, I heard a rustling, and the balcony door opened as someone entered. I sat up and looked at the silhouette, unable to make out his features.

"It's me," he soothed, kneeling on the bed.

"I feared you wouldn't come." I reached toward him, and he held my face in his hands.

"I'll never fail to come for you," he whispered.

His lips found mine unerringly in the darkness. His kisses and light caresses made my worries melt away.

I felt as though I'd never known love until that moment. Though he was gentle, my desire for him reached a strength I could no longer control. I returned his kisses insistently, but he hushed me to a slower pace.

"Please," I begged.

But he just sealed my mouth with a deep kiss.

I throbbed with need, having waited far too long for this. "How can you... I want you right now. Don't you want me?" I swallowed the tears at the back of my throat.

I felt him smile against my lips. "I want you entirely and thoroughly. I want you all to myself. I want your every thought to be of me and your every breath to be for me."

He gently took my hand and led it up his leg. I felt him, long and hard for me, and I gasped.

"You understand?"

I knew he couldn't see me nod, so I leaned in to kiss him again. Then, I challenged him. "You want me thoroughly and entirely? Then take me. Show me you want me so bad it hurts. Take me so completely I can't think of anyone but you, and my every breath will be for you."

He lay me down, stroking my hair. Just as he was leaning in to kiss me again, the moon broke through the clouds.

Soft moonlight filtered into my room, and I looked into the eyes of my lover.

He smiled, and I whispered his name breathlessly as he bent to place another reverent kiss on my lips.

"Jack."

TWENTY-FIVE

I awoke with a feeling of astonishment at what my subconscious mind had dreamt up and a yearning I couldn't quell.

I turned my head toward the door that Jack had come through in my dream. The morning sun filtered through the glass and lit up the dust, which floated around like shimmering specks of wishes yet to be made.

Enchanted, I opened my mouth to make a wish. No words came out.

What do I wish for?

My heart ached as though longing for something just out of reach, a feeling I knew far too well. Yet, this time somehow seemed different.

Many of my wishes are impossible. I wish Cy hadn't died. I wish we hadn't fought, and I wish he hadn't misunderstood my relationship with Jack. Though in light of recent discoveries, I can see why he was self-conscious. But those would be wasted wishes. Even if someone could bring a soul back to life, Cy's has already moved on. Somewhere, he's a small child with a different name and a new life.

Remembering Cy's fiercely cheerful blue eyes when we'd first met, I smiled.

We were about that age when we met. I hope he's enjoying a new childhood and making good friends. I hope this life will be long and happy.

Imagining what Cy was doing in his new life made it difficult for me to be sad. *We may have parted ways on our journeys, but that doesn't mean we'll never see each other again. We still have many lifetimes to live. If we're really meant to be soulmates, then we'll find a way back to each other.*

My vision blurred as bittersweet tears of farewell overflowed, and I cried as if I was trying to get every drop of Cy out of me. I grabbed the tarot card on my nightstand and kissed it softly. Slipping it out of sight into the drawer, I wished Cy the best of luck.

My cleansing cry had washed away the ache I felt for Cy, but it hadn't helped my situation with Jack. My soul felt wrung out and hollow.

After splashing cold water on my face, I stared at my tear-swollen eyes in the mirror. *Hurting Jack is unforgivable. He's loved and supported you for most of your life. Even if you can never return his love, you can't leave it like this. You need to talk to him.*

"You're too cruel," I heard Jack say in my mind.

A sense of dread swooped down on me. *What about Jesse? If Jack finds out about what we did, he'll never forgive me.*

"He's suspicious," Jack told me.

But Jack doesn't know the whole story. Still, even though I know a little more about Jesse, there's a lot I don't know. He remains a mystery.

I shook my head to clear it.

My relationship with Jack is separate from what's going on with Jesse. I'll talk to Jack when I get the chance. As for Jesse, I'll just have to see what happens.

Dad was surprised to see me when I came down to breakfast. He smiled over his cup of tea.

"Anna, my girl, you've been working hard."

"I have."

"Still haven't found your missing fellow, eh?"

"No discussing cases at the table," Aunt Vi scolded as she set plates of eggs and sausage before us.

We apologized without remorse and started eating.

After enjoying our food in silence for a while, Dad asked, "So how's Jackie Boy? You said you were meeting him on Sunday. Didn't you?"

I choked on my coffee, coughing and covering my mouth. Aunt Vi and Dad's brows furrowed, but I held up my other hand to show them I was all right.

Staring regretfully at my half-eaten breakfast, I rose from the table.

"I've got work to do this morning. Thanks for breakfast, Aunt Vi."

Making a quick escape, I pushed down my guilt and regret.

While the sun was so bright that I had to squint to see, the winter wind blew away any warmth it had brought with it. Our street was quiet since most people had already left for work.

I let out a long sigh just to see my frosty breath. My feet knew the way, so I let them take care of it. They led me down a steep, dead-end street. A pub and a small boutique huddled close together among a few bushy evergreens. At the bottom of the hill was a nearly forgotten bookstore with a cat sunning itself in the window.

A bell tinkled as I entered the shop, and the cat stretched and padded over to greet me. Standing on his hind legs, he pawed my thigh. I knelt down and scratched his ears.

"Hey there, Merlin. How have you been? You ready to tell me whether you're really a cat or not?"

Merlin meowed and blinked his large yellow eyes at me before strutting back to his spot on the windowsill.

Fred, a middle-aged witch with a balding gray head and cheaters that almost fell off his spotted nose, stuck his head out from one of the aisles.

"Good morning, Fred."

"Anna," he greeted with a smile and emerged with arms full of books.

"How are you?" I asked.

"Age seems to be catching up to me these days. I can't get the winter chill out of my bones." He set the thick volumes on the counter with loving care.

"You're not that old, Fred."

He chuckled. "You've always been such a kind girl. So what can I help you with today? That old copy of Sherlock Holmes finally given out?"

"No, I take good care of it. I'm actually just passing through today. Do you mind giving me a hand?"

"Out on another adventure, eh?"

I nodded without elaborating, and he motioned for me to follow him.

The bookshelves, packed with dusty old tomes, were set up almost like a maze. I could get lost in any one of the books on his shelves, so I always thought a maze was the perfect setup for Fred's shop. Out of sight of the front door was a shelf filled with folklore and fairy tales.

A hanging lamp illuminated the titles. It looked like a winged dragon with claws that wrapped protectively around the light bulb. His barbed tail whipped behind him, ready to crush anyone who came near.

Fred reached for the tail and twisted it twice with a "click, click."

The bookshelf unlocked, and Fred pushed it open to reveal a set of stone stairs.

"I need to go to Miller's Magical Tools," I told him.

He breathed life into my violet will-o'-the-wisp guide and set it free.

"Thanks, Fred." I smiled at him before descending to Starlight Avenue.

TWENTY-SIX

Miller's Magical Tools was in a tunnel crowded with doors to witch shops. Wondering what their topside covers were, I entered after my guide.

The brightly-lit basement was neatly organized. Glass cases sat in rows, proudly displaying the wares. Rings and necklaces with sparkling, polished stones shined beside artfully carved wands and sharp knives with ornate handles.

The "clank, clank, clank" of hammering metal on metal echoed from the floor above, and the inescapable scent of burning coal made my nostrils flare and my eyes water.

A man sat at a workbench in the corner, carefully removing the bark from a stick. He didn't seem to notice my presence as he stripped the wood.

"Excuse me," I interrupted softly, not wanting to startle him.

"Be right with you," he called, not looking up from his work.

After a few moments, he set down the wand-to-be and looked up at me.

His mismatched eyes crinkled in the corners when he smiled through day-old stubble. His slacks and the front of his flannel shirt were sprinkled with woodchips.

"How can I help you?"

"I'm here to ask about Charlie Miller," I explained apologetically.

His smile disappeared, and his mismatched eyes turned cold.

"It's been five years since my brother was murdered. I've already told the coppers everything I know."

"I'm sure it's painful to talk about," I sympathized. "I'm a private detective. The man I was hired to find may have disappeared in the same way as your brother. I want to find him before anything happens. Won't you help me save a life?"

He sighed in the face of my pleading. "What do you want to know?"

"Thank you."

He nodded while crossing his arms.

"It's my understanding your brother was acting strangely before he disappeared."

"Yeah, Charlie was always dead focused when it came to work. He was a blacksmith and made ceremonial daggers and the like. It takes a lot of strength and discipline to do that kind of work, but Charlie lived for it. Shortly before his disappearance, he seemed distracted. He didn't have the motivation to work, and the things he did make lacked his usual excellence."

"Do you have any idea why he was acting that way?"

His eyes drifted away from me as he hesitated. "Charlie had a peculiar preference when it came to relationships."

"Do you mean to say your brother preferred men?" I asked gently.

He nodded. "It's difficult for people like Charlie. He seemed to have given up on relationships a long time before. But shortly before his disappearance, he said he'd met someone."

"Do you know anything about this man?"

"No, I wish I would've asked Charlie more about him. I only know he was human."

Lizzie said Leo's lover was a witch. "What happened the day your brother disappeared?"

"He was supposed to help Laura, our younger sister. She's the one pounding upstairs. Charlie was teaching her blacksmithing, and he was supposed to meet her at the shop that day. He didn't come when he'd said he would. We checked his room when we got home, but it looked like he'd just packed up and left. We didn't understand at first. We thought he'd just run away without saying goodbye. They found him dead two weeks later. We still don't know what happened to him," he finished bitterly.

"I'm sorry."

"It's not like the coppers care about a few murdered witches," he spat.

There wasn't anything I could say to that. *He's right. The police don't care about witches. They're the minority and, since prohibition, they see them as the main perpetrators of crime. What can a human like me do to empathize with him? I've never experienced injustice like he has.*

"It's not much consolation, but there are those who're still working in support of the magical community."

He sighed again. "I know. We just want justice for our brother, same as everyone else."

"Even if your brother's case has nothing to do with the one I'm working. I'll look into these Phantom murders."

Giving me a tired smile, he nodded. "Thanks."

Mr. Miller walked me to the back door and created my guide to The Emerald Herbalist.

The guide led me to a ladder, which climbed up to a trapdoor. I ascended into a pantry, where shelves were crowded with jars of bizarre dried and pickled plants the likes of which I'd never seen before.

After leaving the pantry through a Dutch door, I entered an herbal tea and plant shop. The back of the shop had jars of recognizable dried herbs and spices. Overhead, bundles of herbs were hanging as they dried. The front half of the shop felt more like a conservatory. Florae grew in pots, on shelves, or in hanging baskets. There was even a fountain with seaweed and water lilies. The street was barely visible through all of the leaves soaking up the sun in the front window.

A thin woman with frizzy hair and thick coke bottle cheaters talked to the plants while watering them.

"I'm so glad the sun came out for you today. I know you were getting depressed from not seeing it for a while," she told them.

I stifled a giggle and tried to keep a solemn face. "Ma'am?"

"Yes, dear, I'm coming," she answered in a sing-song voice. She flitted over to me and raised her eyebrows expectantly.

I felt bad that I was about to ruin her good mood. "My name is Anna Caill. I'm a private detective."

Her sadness seemed to make even her hair droop. "You're here to ask about Catherine."

I nodded.

She shuffled over to a counter and poured us each a small cup of lukewarm, chamomile tea. I drank it with her, allowing her time to collect her thoughts.

"Has someone hired you to find the Phantom?" she asked, finally breaking the silence.

"Not exactly. Another witch has gone missing, but I'm not sure whether it's related to the Phantom case or not."

"So you want me to tell you about Catherine to see if it's related to your case?"

"Yes, but I'm also planning to look into the Phantom murders when my case is solved."

She smiled softly. "My daughter, Catherine, was a bright, free-spirited girl. She was always happy and planning one of her adventures. She traveled all over, bringing back seeds or plants for the shop. Sometimes, she didn't tell me when she was going, so I wasn't worried when she disappeared. But when they found her..." Her voice gave out.

"Had she been acting strangely before her disappearance?"

"She seemed more contemplative than usual. She'd stare off with a blank look, but then again, she was always a daydreamer."

"Did she say anything about a new man in her life?"

"She mentioned she'd met someone interesting while gathering herbs in the country. She started going out there more frequently. Sometimes, she'd come home and say she'd seen him."

"Do you know anything about him?"

She shook her head. "Catherine commonly met interesting people on her journeys. I suppose it was more suspicious that she didn't talk about him in detail."

"Did she mention whether he was a witch or human?"

"No."

"Do you know... Was she intimate with this man?"

She shrugged. "Possibly. She didn't usually tell me that

type of information. However, I got the impression that if they weren't, they soon would be."

I suppose there are people who're interested in both men and women.

"Thank you for the tea and talking with me today. I may return when I'm looking further into the Phantom case."

TWENTY-SEVEN

B ack at home, I took off my hat and coat and went to Dad's study. As expected, he sat by the fire reading the day's newspaper. I flopped into the armchair next to his.

"Did you read the paper today? Jack wrote a story about the streetcar men threatening to strike." He looked over the daily, saw my face, and folded it. "The investigation doesn't seem to be going well."

"I've run out of leads. I don't even know where to look next," I whined, slouching into the chair.

"I'm not hearing my girl give up. Am I?" he challenged.

"Other than staking out the gin joint the high priest and his lover visited, I don't know where else to look."

He folded his hands over his belly and stared at me until I met his gaze. "You need to separate what you know from what you don't know. You're so far into it that you're all turned around. So what do you know?"

I took a deep breath and let it out all at once. "I know Mr. Nimzic hasn't been acting like himself lately, and he has a new male lover only Lizzie knew about. I know this lover is a witch with blond hair, and they met at a bar called Erostes. I also know the lover frequents The Shadow Market. On the day he disappeared, I know Mr. Nimzic met with Lizzie to tell her he was naming her his successor. Then, he went home to wait for his lover to call him on the telephone. I know he had planned to meet Jesse later that night at The Black Moon, but he never showed."

"Was there anything unusual or out of place at his home?"

"Mr. Nimzic appears to be an incredibly clean and organized person, but his bedroom looked as if he'd packed in a hurry. I know he left with his lover instead of meeting Jesse because his neighbor saw them. Other than a messy bedroom, three other things seemed out of place: the magical seal that protects him and his home was broken, the picture of Rose was turned down, and there was a charm bag under his bed. Jesse told me the charm bag was to help with nightmares but thought some of the ingredients might lead us to where his friend has been recently. Most likely, the photo was turned down because he'd recently broken up with Rose to be with his lover. Rose didn't seem upset, and she was pretty tight-lipped when I talked to her. Ace looked into any connection with The Druzina and found none. Jack gave me some articles about a possible mass murderer, known as the Phantom, who has been snatching and killing witches for years. I talked to two of the victims' family members, and one of them said the victim was seeing a human, not a witch. Either the Phantom murders are unrelated to their lovers, or there is a witch and a human out there working together. There is no way a regular human could take on a witch alone. The likelihood that there is a multiple-victim murderer out there is improbable. And the thought that two could be working together? It's so unheard of that I have to put it down as impossible. As such, I don't think Mr. Nimzic's case and the Phantom are related. Odds are, Mr. Nimzic started acting strangely because he was pursuing a socially unacceptable romance, and he and his lover just ran off together. People run away with their lovers every day."

Dad nodded his agreement with my assessment. "So what don't you know?"

"I don't know where Mr. Nimzic and his lover went or why he didn't cancel his appointment with Jesse. I don't know why or by whom his seal was broken or if it was just accidental damage. I don't know what Rose is hiding, and I don't know if Jesse has looked into the charm bag's unusual ingredients, or if they are even useful."

"Then, you know what you have to do next?"

I smiled. "I'm going to question Rose again."

He beamed with pride. "That's my girl."

As I stood to kiss him on the head, he began coughing. It continued longer than usual, and my stomach clenched when I heard how wet it sounded. I grabbed the glass of water from the table beside him as I helplessly waited for the fit to end.

When he was ready, he accepted the glass from me, and I closed my eyes at the red-tinged mucus in his palm.

"I'm fine." He smiled weakly after sipping the water. He waved his hand for me to leave. "Go on. You have work to do. I'll be here for you to tell me all about it once you solve the case."

I left him alone and closed the doors behind me. Leaning my back against them, I shut my eyes and took a few shaky breaths to calm myself.

After settling my nerves, I went to the telephone to ring Maggie.

"Private detective, Anna Caill's office."

"Maggie, it's me. I know you're about to head home for the day. Do you have any messages for me?"

"Oh hey, Anna! Nope, no messages."

I hesitated. "Did Jack call at all today?"

"Jack? No, he didn't. Were you expecting a call? Aw, I don't have to stay late. Do I?"

My heart sank. "No. Thanks, Maggie. That's not necessary," I said, trying not to sound down. "Have a good night."

"You too, Anna."

Next, I called The Black Moon, and the bartender answered.

"Yes, this is Anna Caill. I came in the other day with Jesse Hunt to see Rose."

I could hear his smile. "I remember you."

"I found something of Rose's, and I know she'd want it right away. Would you mind giving me her address so I can drop it off to her?"

"Why don't you ask Hunt? He's taken her home before."

"I would, but what I've found is sensitive you see. I don't want to tell him about it if she doesn't want me to."

"I understand. Hold on a second while I get it."

"Thank you."

He gave me the address and told me he'd buy me a drink the next time I came in. I promised to see him again with no plans to do so.

I telephoned Jesse next. His smooth voice caressed my skin and quickened my pulse.

"Hello?"

"Jesse? It's Anna. I've got good news."

"You've found Leo?"

Discouraged, I replied less enthusiastically. "No, but it

doesn't seem the Phantom murders have anything to do with Mr. Nimzic's case."

"That's a relief at least."

"Yeah, so I've got one more lead to follow. I'll come to your place tomorrow and let you in on the rest."

He hummed his agreement, and it reminded me of his hot breath in my ear. I shivered, struggling to remind myself that I needed to find out more about him, not be attracted to his mystery.

"Okay, tomorrow then," I said.

He hummed again and cut the line.

Before I could lose my nerve, I made one more call.

"*The Times*, Jack O'Keefe speaking."

"Hey," I said weakly.

"Anna?"

"Yeah, it's me."

He paused for a while, and I worried that he'd hung up. Finally, he said, "Listen, Anna, I'm really busy right now."

"I understand. When should I call back?"

"I don't know... I need to work some things out first. I'll call you when I'm ready. All right?"

With a click, the line went dead. I bit my lip and hung up the earpiece. Fighting the burning at the back of my nose, I shuffled toward the stairs and managed to make it to my room before I burst into tears.

TWENTY-EIGHT

I awoke early the next morning with swollen eyes and a throbbing headache. *I feel like I've cried more in the past six days than I have in the past six years.*

The light through my balcony door was a weak predawn gray, and no wish dust floated in my room. Though I didn't dream the night before, I still didn't feel rested. My body ached as if I had lain twisted in the same uncomfortable position for too long.

My red, puffy face in the mirror told me cosmetics were a must.

I ate a quick breakfast of bread and cheese in the kitchen and left before Dad and Aunt Vi were even awake.

The train and streetcar I took to Rose's were sparsely occupied by tired-looking people heading home after the late shift. One man slept with his cheek pressed against the glass and drool trickling down his chin.

Rose's apartment building was a women's tenant house. The grime on the outside looked like chocolate icing on a melting birthday cake. It seemed to paste the building into the gloomy neighborhood. The inside, however, was as clean as the old fixtures would allow.

I climbed the narrow stairs to the fourth floor and knocked on the door marked "41."

A brunette in her early twenties answered in her dressing gown with rags still in her hair and her cosmetics not yet applied.

"What's the big idea knockin' at someone's doa' this urly in the mornin'?" she demanded.

While it was early, only people who'd stayed out all night would still be in bed.

"I'm here to see Rose," I explained to her roommate.

She clicked her tongue at me. "And is she expectin' you?" she asked in a high hatty tone.

"Probably not, but she'll see me anyway."

"Oh, will she? Hey, Rose," she called loudly over her shoulder. "Some tomata's hea' ta see ya."

Rose appeared, also in her dressing gown, over her roommate's shoulder. Her cold eyes squinted at me. "What do _you_ want?"

"I've some more questions."

"I already told ya I don't know nothin'." She crossed her arms resolutely.

"Then, I guess you've nothing to hide. Why not just let me ask my questions, you can tell me you don't know, and I'll be on my way?"

She squinted, thinking about my proposition. "Yeah, all right."

She opened the door wider for me, and I followed her into a lush apartment that didn't rightly fit into the old building. Rich rugs squished beneath my shoes while I took in the art and furniture that looked like it had been donated by a wealthy patron.

"Give us a minute, Amelia," Rose instructed while turning to face me.

Amelia nodded and retreated down the hall.

Neither of us sat on the cream-colored furniture. I stared into Rose's stony composure.

"I'll make this quick," I started.

"Please do."

I didn't acknowledge her unnecessary comment. "I'm having a hard time locating Mr. Nimzic. Since you were seeing each other, I imagine you'd know him best."

She didn't respond.

"How long were you and Mr. Nimzic together?"

"Just over six months." Her expression gave nothing away.

"That's quite a while. You must've been upset when he broke up with you."

She pursed her lips but didn't say anything.

"Do you have any idea where he'd go with a lover?"

She sniffed in disdain. "No, we neva' went outta town."

This isn't going anywhere. I need to figure out how to elicit a reaction. "Were you intimate with Mr. Nimzic at all?"

"I don't see how that's any a' yoa' business."

"Well, I'm just curious how you wouldn't know your lover is a homosexual. I mean, unless men not responding to you is the norm."

Her face went red. Nevertheless, she remained silent.

"Jesse told me he introduced you and Mr. Nimzic. Is that correct?"

Her eyes widened when I used his given name, but she nodded.

"I imagine he's upset you two broke up. It's difficult for friends when a couple splits. Especially the kind of break up you had with him two-timing you and all. There will inevitably be hard feelings, and friends sometimes choose sides. I wonder who Jesse feels more loyalty toward. When he found out Mr. Nimzic was cheating, he didn't even get angry. I believe he said something like 'I don't want to judge him too harshly.'"

"What do you know about Jesse anyway?" she shot back angrily. "You ain't nobody. Yoa' jus' the hired help."

I smirked at her, gratified that I'd gotten a reaction. "People meet in all kinds of ways."

The blood drained from her face. "What ah ya sayin'?"

"I'm saying that a relationship can start out one way and change into something else. You never know what could happen."

She gritted her teeth and hissed, "He wouldn't."

I smiled pleasantly. "He already did."

It seemed to take a moment for her to process my words. When she did, she screamed like a kettle letting off steam.

"The dirty rat thinks he's gonna play me?" she muttered, laughing to herself as she paced the room.

Her head snapped in my direction, and her eyes glared at me. "Ya think yoa' so smawt. Dontcha? Ya think ya got it all figud out, an' Jesse's gonna keep all thos' sweet promises he whispud in the dawk. You don't know nothin' about Jesse Hunt. Alls he cairs about is himself. He told ya he introduced Leo to me? You bet he did! He told me to seduce Leo so's he could get his mitts on the coven's book a shadas. He even broke Leo's seal so's we could cast spells on 'im if we needed ta. He shows me a love chawm and asks if it's mine? He's got to be jokin' me! Like I'd eva' need such dirty tricks like that to get a man. And Leo? There's no way he's a fairy. I could barely beat him offa me. I don't know what's goin' on with him, but he ain't got no male lova'. Let me give ya a piece of advice, Doll.

Neva' fall in love with a man ya can't predict, an' stay clea' of weasels like Jesse Hunt."

I managed to walk out of Rose's apartment in one piece, but the sound of shattering slammed the other side of the door as I closed it.

Though my stomach turned at the thought of Jesse fooling me, my mind sighed with relief. I felt reassured. All of the bits I couldn't figure out, and the way Jesse acted after he'd had me in the palm of his hand, finally made sense.

What Rose had said had given me a general idea. Still, the details weren't clear. I sucked on my teeth and balled my fists as anger urged me toward the rat in question.

TWENTY-NINE

Jesse answered his door looking just as enticing as usual, and I was pleased to see my body didn't respond pleasantly.

His calculating gaze must've noticed my suppressed anger because the distant expression he'd been showing me since I'd foolishly given myself to him melted into a warm smile.

"Good morning." He leaned against the doorframe, oozing charm. I wasn't buying it.

I pushed past him without a word.

He closed the door and met my eyes with concern. "Is everything all right?"

"Just tell me one thing," I fumed, my anger bubbling just below the surface. "Did you use magic to seduce me? Did you cast a spell on me?"

Jesse clicked his tongue and rolled his eyes. "Do you honestly think I even needed to waste the power? You've been panting for me since the moment we met. A smile here, a sad story there, you didn't make it difficult."

Balling up my hands, I shook with fury.

He chuckled bitterly. "Are you disillusioned now that mysterious, intriguing, sad little Jesse isn't who you'd imagined him to be?"

He stepped closer to me, but I stood my ground. "Or do you like this better?" he whispered. "I bet you'd still beg for me to be inside you even now."

I gave him a right hook in his smug face. My hand throbbed, but nothing cracked, and my rage dulled the pain.

Jesse sucked his teeth and spit a little blood onto the floor of his living room. Unfortunately, I didn't seem to have hurt him badly because he just looked irritated.

Jack was right. I need answers. "So you're the one who broke Leo's seal?"

"Yeah, and?"

"You convinced Rose to seduce him to get to the coven's book of shadows?"

"Well, it never hurts to have someone on the inside." He sighed and shook his head, disappointed. "I should've known Rose wasn't a good choice."

Impatient to get more information while he was still being candid, I asked, "And Martin?"

"The old man was so trusting. The moment he told me about the book of shadows, I knew I had to become his successor at all costs. I didn't even have to wait long after he performed the private succession ritual. He graciously died before the public naming, and I told the coven the artifacts were lost."

"Did he really die of natural causes?"

Jesse curled his lip as if disgusted by my insinuation. "He did."

"All this for a book?"

He sighed. "A book of *shadows*: a book containing all the wisdom and spells collected by a coven since its formation."

"Is that why you befriended Mr. Nimzic?"

"An inexperienced witch with one of the oldest books of shadows in existence? How could I resist? Once he named me his successor, I'd have access to the book and could steal it at any time. I do like Leo, but he's surprisingly gullible. I guess I should've known someone else would've seen it, too."

"His lover."

"I was astonished when you said Leo was a homosexual. I thought that love charm was put under his bed by Rose. Now, I'm sure it was put there by this male lover of his."

I snorted. "The charm for nightmares."

He smirked.

"Why're you trying so hard to find him when you aren't really friends?"

"At first, I didn't want the book lost before he could name me his successor. I didn't know he wasn't planning on choosing me. Now, I hope rescuing him will ensure he names me instead of that brat Lizzie. Besides, I was a suspect, and I'm not taking the fall for something I didn't do. And of course, it's a matter of pride. How dare someone snatch the subject of my long scam right from under me?"

"Patrick suspected you."

"Thanks for that information by the way. I knew you were keeping things from me, but I didn't know what. My intuition is highly developed. I always know just what to say or do to get what I want." He smiled at me suggestively, and I gagged. "I didn't mind indulging you in order to loosen your lips, but I couldn't let you get too close. I'm sorry I brushed you away so coldly. What do you say? I'll let you start where I stopped you before."

"Do it yourself," I spat, disgusted. "I've got work to do. Mr. Nimzic is an innocent victim, and I'm going to save him from you and his snatcher."

He sobered. "And what do you plan to do?"

"I'll use the hair in the charm found under his bed to identify who this fella is."

"I knew you were clever, but how do you expect to do that? You told me Patrick said their whereabouts were cloaked."

"I have informants. I'm sure they'll know where I can find someone who can get around it."

"Cloaking spells are strong magic. I doubt anyone less than a coven leader could see through them."

I bit my lip, not wanting to ask for his help. "What do you suggest?" I growled.

"After Rose said the charm wasn't hers, I started looking into it. I promised you I would after all," he congratulated himself. "The black powder included with the hair? I just found out who sells it and where to find him."

"Nifty, give it to me, and I'll question him."

He shook his head. "I don't think so. I'm going, too."

"The Hell you are."

"He's at The Shadow Market. How are you going to get in?"

"What good are you? You barely got in last time alone."

He snorted.

"And that was just a lie so I wouldn't suspect you."

"I won't tell you where to go if you don't let me come along."

"You'd let Leo die?"

"You mean *you'd* let Leo die."

I ground my teeth, and he smiled triumphantly.

"Fine, let's go."

THIRTY

Rather than entering The Shadow Market through Erostes, Jesse parked on the street in front of a wide, brick building on the corner of Walnut and Perkins. The artist's studio was open with high ceilings, polished wood floors, and stark white walls.

Jesse hoofed through the gallery with the confidence of someone who knew where he was going. Every twenty feet or so, an oil painting hung. We passed paintings of a drugstore and a lighthouse on a hill. I stopped to appreciate one of a woman drinking tea as the lights of the deserted café reflected off the dark window behind her.

Jesse looked over his shoulder when he realized I wasn't following him. "Pick up your feet," he scolded me.

I tore my eyes away from the lonely scene, hoping the woman found comfort in her warm drink.

Turning a corner, we saw a man mostly hidden by a sketchbook. He drew intently, not noticing our presence at all.

"We're headed through, Ed," Jesse called to him.

He waved his hand without replying.

The dark, narrow hallway that led to creaky, wooden stairs was in severe contrast to the bright openness of the studio.

A solid woman with dark hair plaited down her back stood by the door at the bottom of the stairs.

"Jo," Jesse greeted with a nod.

She didn't respond but let us pass into Starlight Avenue.

Jesse created our guide. But instead of the usual violet, it was bright green.

"Why's it a different color?" I couldn't stop myself from asking.

He smirked as if he enjoyed my curiosity getting the better of me. "You didn't think the spell to get to The Shadow Market would be the same. Did you?"

I averted my eyes, regretting opening my mouth.

We followed the green will-o'-the-wisp through the dark tunnels to an iron gate with a crystal orb embedded in it. The guide floated into the orb, which lit up brightly. The gate clicked open, and we went through before it slammed behind us with an echoing clang.

As we continued, the tunnel seemed even colder and darker than before. A shadow moved through the air like ink in water. Fear shivered up my spine, and I shamelessly moved closer to Jesse.

When the shadow had entirely blocked out all the light but a dim glimmer, he pulled something from his coat pocket and flung his hand out. There was the sound of liquid splashing on stone, and the inky shadow slunk away. Light illuminated our path once more.

"What was that?" I asked as Jesse slipped an empty vial back into his pocket.

"A sacrifice."

"Do I want to know?"

"Probably not."

Finally, we came to a thick, wooden door guarded by two men who towered over us and looked as though they could crush us with their bare hands. As we approached, they tensed. "Who's the woman?" the baby grand on the left demanded in a deep growl.

"She's with me," Jesse asserted, unperturbed.

The guards exchanged glances. "Will she be returning by herself at a later time?" the guard on the right asked.

"No, you need not worry about adding her to the system."

They nodded and stepped aside.

The Shadow Market was in a giant cavern. Dangerous rock spikes threatened to impale us from above, and an eerie green light illuminated the entire market from a wall of crystal clusters.

From the top of the hill we stood on, we looked out at the market below. Tents were set up in disorganized rows like those of a small town. There seemed to be caves that branched off from the main cavern, though the entrances were covered with cloth, so it was hard to say.

I followed Jesse down the slippery, uneven steps to the crowded lanes. We wound through the tents and ducked into one of dark green canvas with a torn roof.

There were wooden shelves filled with jars and tins. A red-headed witch with a button nose and scraggly facial hair sat at a table grinding something with a mortar and pestle.

He looked up as we entered, and his eyes widened.

"Arthur, isn't it? How are you today?" Jesse asked pleasantly while strolling toward him.

"Y-you're J-Jesse Hunt."

"I'm pleased there's no need for introductions."

"H-how can I h-help you, J-Jesse?" Arthur's eyes darted around, looking anywhere but at him.

Jesse leaned onto Arthur's table and peeked into the mortar. "That powder you're grinding, it's used in love spells. Correct?"

Arthur shivered but nodded.

"It's a proprietary blend. Is it not? Your powder is the only one in The Shadow Market that's black?"

"It's p-particularly potent for sexual obsession. I'd be happy to g-give you a d-deal, Jesse."

Jesse's lips curled. "I don't need such means to get what I want," Jesse said, disgusted. "Isn't that right, Anna?" he added more pleasantly.

I clenched my jaw.

"Of c-course not, Jesse," Arthur covered, his teeth chattering.

"I'm looking for a customer of yours: a blond man with a red scarf. He bought some of your powder."

Arthur's eyes flickered in recognition.

"Who is it?" Jesse demanded politely.

"C-come on, Jesse. You know t-the rules. W-we're supposed to k-keep our c-customers confidential."

Jesse reached across the table and grabbed Arthur by the collar. He slammed his head on the table and snapped his fingers in front of Arthur's face. After a few muttered words, his fingers sparked, and he held a fireball in his palm. The flame danced menacingly in Arthur's blue eyes.

"Who is it?" Jesse asked again, much less pleasantly.

"T-two witches," Arthur screamed. "It started with a black-haired witch with black eyes named Raven. After a few years, he brought the blond with him. He goes by Fjolnir."

"Fjolnir? As in Odin?" Jesse asked.

I flinched at the name. "Odin? The Norse god?"

"Y-yes."

The gears in my mind started to spin out of control. I ran to the table and slammed both palms onto it.

"Do you know if there's a way to turn a human into a witch?"

Arthur blinked at my question. I looked at Jesse, who shrugged.

The red-head remained silent, so Jesse shook him and brought the fire closer to his face. "Answer her."

"Yes! Yes! There's a way, but it's serious dark magic. You could do it through a combination of blood and sex magic."

My heart stopped. I ran out of the tent without a word, feeling like movement was the only way to cope.

Jesse yelled and chased after me, but I just kept running. Eventually, I cornered myself where the green crystalline glow reflected off a still, dark pool.

Jesse grabbed my wrist to stop me from running again.

"I know who it is," I whispered between heaving breaths.

"You do? Then, let's go."

"I don't know how to find them."

"What're you saying?"

"There's no way to know where they are… short of the Registry."

"Only witches with pure intentions can use the Registry. There has to be another way." For the first time, I saw fear creep into Jesse's eyes.

"If I'm right, then Leo is in serious danger. He may even be dead already."

"The kind of magic Arthur was spilling about is best done on the full or dark moon," Jesse mused.

"When's the next full or dark moon?"

"The full moon is tomorrow." Jesse paced back and forth. "It's not worth the risk. I'd rather let Leo die."

"You coward. What about the sense of pride you were so worried about?"

"It's not worth getting vaporized if the Registry thinks my motive isn't pure enough!"

I sighed, defeated. "Then, Leo is doomed."

Jesse froze in his tracks and turned to me. "There's one way that might work."

I could already tell what he was going to say by the look in his eyes. "No, no way. I'm not taking a blood oath with you."

"It's standard when a human asks a witch to risk his life."

"You wanted to find him, too."

"Besides, mixing our blood would mean the Registry would pick up on your pure intentions."

"But then I'd owe you a blood debt. I'm not going to effectively be your slave until it's paid."

"Those are my conditions. I wasn't lying when I said you were clever. I could really use your help to further my purposes, and I find that I'm...growing rather fond of you," he admitted as if forced.

"Not happening." In the distance, I saw the stairs that led to the Erostes exit. I started hiking toward it without another word.

"Leo doesn't have much time. Are you really going to leave him to die? When you change your mind, I'll be waiting at my place." Jesse called after me, but I didn't turn around.

THIRTY-ONE

Too many thoughts spun in my head, and my feet seemed to move on their own. Crushed under an oppressive weight, my heart sought the one comfort it could always rely on.

I wound up at Jack's door with only a foggy recollection of how I'd gotten there. The fact that Jack had told me not to contact him wasn't even considered as I knocked.

There was no answer.

I don't have time for you to ignore me, Jack. I pulled out my lockpick and let myself in. His apartment was quiet and dark. *I guess he wasn't ignoring me after all. He isn't home.*

The clock told me Jack should've been home a while before. I sat on his couch in the dark, determined to wait for him.

Chilled with fear and anxiety, I wrapped a blanket around my shoulders and slumped to one side, curling into a ball. My mind wouldn't rest, thinking about all that had happened, Jesse's offer, and what would happen next.

Warm and wrapped in Jack's comforting scent, I eventually fell into an exhausted sleep. I awoke the next morning to overcast light filtering through the windows. Realizing what had happened, I bolted upright.

"Jack?" I called into the still apartment.

I threw off the blanket and investigated. His kitchen and bedroom looked as undisturbed as they had the night before.

Jack never came home. I hope he's all right. He may have been working on a story or slept at the office. In that case, he probably won't come home until later.

I went to Jack's desk in search of a pencil and paper to leave him a note. A journal and pen were all that sat on his desk. Opening the drawer for loose paper, I gasped and froze at the incomprehensible sight. My hand shook as I pulled out the periwinkle ribbon.

"He already cherishes something of yours," the fortune teller's voice echoed in my mind.

The edges of the ribbon were slightly frayed from being handled. Otherwise, it looked the same as when I'd lost it at the carnival.

"The crystal was never mine. I won it with the purpose of giving it to Cy. But the ribbon…Jack…" I whispered.

Tears trickled down my face, and I looked through them to the journal on his desk. I knew I probably shouldn't, but I didn't even waver as I opened it and flipped through the pages. When I saw my name, I stopped at a page dated a few days before.

"I finally told Anna how I feel about her. My heart overflowed, and we kissed. I was so sure she was going to accept my feelings. She returned my kisses with a desperate passion that matched my own. It's strange that Cy seems more of an obstacle in death than he ever was alive. I know I shouldn't speak ill of the dead, but jealousy still

darkens my memories of him. I don't know if I can ever forgive him for ignoring my love for her. He knew how I felt long before she ever confessed to him. I should've told her of what the carnival fortune teller promised so long ago. As her soulmate, I have to be understanding. I have to have faith she will find her way to me one day. I know we belong to each other. She will always be mine and I hers no matter who comes between us. But truthfully, I cannot feel hope right now. I feel only pain. My chest aches with every heartbeat, and I feel so cold since she left my arms. Is this what the rest of my life will be like?"

The journal slipped through my fingers as my heart wrenched and heavy sobs split my throat. I fell to my knees, unable to support my own weight. *I need to talk to him.*

Clutching the wet, crumpled ribbon, I stumbled to the telephone. It took a few deep breaths to steady my shaking hands as I dialed the rotary.

"*The Times*, how may I direct your call?" the switchboard operator answered.

"I need to speak to Jack O'Keefe."

"I'm sorry, Miss. Mr. O'Keefe is out. Can I take a message?"

"Do you know when he'll be back?"

"I'm sorry. I don't. Do you have a message for him?"

"No, thank you."

I hung up the earpiece and returned to Jack's desk. Sitting in his chair, I grabbed a pen and paper and froze. *There's so much to say. I don't know where to begin.* I thought about what he needed to know and what I was going to do next. *I'm scared, and I wanted to talk this through with Jack. What would he say if he were here? He'd hold me and tell me he was beside me, so I shouldn't be afraid. Even if he isn't here, Jack's always with me. But there has to be another way besides a blood oath with Jesse. Benji? He can't really be found on short notice. He always seems to find me, and I wouldn't want to risk his safety if things go wrong.*

Lillian? No, she'd never agree. We aren't that close. I need to face that murdering liar and save Leo before he's next. If the price is a blood debt to Jesse, so be it. I don't have any other choice. Still, I wish Jack could be there with me.

I wrote, *"I've cracked the case. The only way to catch the culprit is to go to the Registry. I hope you get this soon and will meet me there. With all of my love, your Anna."*

I pressed a kiss to the periwinkle ribbon and placed it on top of the note on his desk.

After washing my face, I hurried to Jesse's apartment.

"All right," I told him while stepping into his living room. "Let's go save Leo."

He bid me follow him to his bedroom. Lighting the candles, it reminded me of the last time I was in his room. I squirmed while thinking of Jack. *He'll forgive me. I know he will.*

We both stepped up to the small altar in the corner. He grabbed a ceremonial knife and held the blade to his left palm.

"I make this blood oath of my own free will. I enter it to fulfill the agreed upon terms. I will use my blood to access the Registry."

Jesse cut his palm and handed me the knife. Following his lead, I held it to my left palm.

"I make this blood oath of my own free will. I enter it to fulfill the agreed upon terms. As you will risk your life to access the Registry, I will be in your debt until such time that…" I stalled.

Jesse urged me with his eyes.

"My debt will be cleared when I save your life." I hissed as the knife slashed my palm.

He held out his left hand, which dripped blood on the floor. Meeting his eyes, I clasped his hand with mine. As he said words of magic while we exchanged blood, I felt as though an invisible chain formed between us. With our blood bond forged, we washed and bound our wounds before leaving.

The drive to the Bureau of Witches Affairs wasn't far, but it took a while because of downtown traffic. I nervously tapped my toe and tried not to think about what the day would bring. I filled my mind with all my happy memories of Jack and his warm embrace and mentally kicked myself for not seeing the truth sooner.

The Bureau of Witches Affairs looked like most government buildings: the imposing columns, the vaulted ceilings, and the echo of footsteps off the marble floors and walls. Records was down the wide, white stairs.

A Trotzky librarian at the front desk of Records looked over her gilded cheaters as we entered.

"How may I help you?" she asked in a raspy voice.

"I need to access the Registry," Jesse explained.

She gave him a stern look then retrieved a stack of papers from a desk drawer.

"Please fill out these liability forms and return them notarized."

"Notarized? Are you serious? You can watch me fill them out right here."

"But I'm not a notary," she said blandly.

Jesse sighed. "Is there a notary in this building?"

"Mr. Walsh on the third floor in Legal is a notary."

"Fine."

As Jesse started for the stairs, I told him I'd wait in Records. *Jack may arrive at any time.* I sat impatiently on a cold, hard bench near the stairs, hoping Jack would come before Jesse returned.

An hour later, Jesse came back with an exasperated expression. "There was a line," he explained. "I don't know how anyone could go through that process and still enter the Registry with pure intentions."

He handed the stack of papers to the librarian, who checked each one meticulously. Jesse drummed his fingers with annoyance, and I kept looking over my shoulder for Jack.

"Everything seems to be in order, Mr. Hunt. You may enter the Registry. It's down the hall on the right." The librarian pointed finally.

The Registry was a thick book, which rested on a pedestal at the center of a glass room. It looked so innocuous sitting there by itself.

Jesse took a few deep breaths, and then he met my eyes. "Kiss for luck?"

"Forget it."

He gave me an almost sad smile. "I'll never forget."

"Just go."

He slipped through the glass door and stepped up to the Registry.

The location of every living witch's soul is in that book. They may have blocked Leo's location from scrying, but they can't fool the Registry.

Placing his hands on the pages of the Registry, Jesse spoke words of magic. The book started to glow, and Jesse threw his head back, facing the ceiling. His eyes were closed, and he started to convulse and mumble.

I pressed my palms to the glass as I helplessly watched from outside. The glass was warm as though the book gave off heat.

Suddenly, the light disappeared, and Jesse crumbled to the floor.

Unsure of what would happen to a human who got too close to the Registry, I banged on the glass and yelled at Jesse.

Eventually, he stirred, and I sighed in relief, knowing he was alive. He managed to crawl to the door, and I helped him to a nearby bench. As he pressed his face to the cool stone of the bench, I knelt beside it.

After a while, his breathing quieted, and he opened his eyes. "I know where he is."

THIRTY-TWO

It was afternoon by the time we made our way back to the librarian, but at least Jesse was upright and walking on his own.

Before we left, I stopped at her desk. "Excuse me. Has a man in his late twenties, a little over six feet, with dark hair stopped by looking for me?"

Her bland stare over her cheaters was my answer. I grabbed a small piece of paper and a pencil from her desk. "If he does come looking for me, please give him this address. His name is Jack, and I'm Anna."

She took my note without a word, and I prayed she'd actually give it to him.

The downtown traffic made our drive out of the city slow and painful. When we finally sped through the suburbs, heavy clouds let loose the white tufts I'd been wishing for only days before. However, the wind slowed our pace much more than the snow. As we burst free of the suburbs, I felt helplessly lost as I took in the open fields of the countryside. It felt like we were searching for something small in an abyss.

Clutching the roadmap, I navigated the route, growing more anxious with every mile. By the time we turned onto the final road, snow covered the ground. Jesse pulled off into a group of trees at the side of the road a quarter of a mile from a small farmhouse with a big barn.

We burrowed into our coats, and I shoved the revolver from my handbag into my pocket.

The snow wasn't falling fast enough to cover our tracks, but the sun was hugging the horizon. The cold wind whipped our faces, and my eyelashes froze when my eyes watered.

"Do you think we can rescue Leo before the ritual starts?" I asked Jesse.

"I don't know. The moon has already risen. They can start the ritual at any time. If I were conducting an elaborate ritual where I was planning to kill someone, I'd start early to have time to deal with the body."

"That makes sense. We'd better hurry."

Closing in on the farmhouse, we snuck up to one side and peered through the window. The bedroom was dark, and nothing stirred. We peeked into all the windows we could reach, but no one was inside. I silently pointed toward the barn. Jesse nodded, and we moved as quickly and quietly as we could. The wind covered the sounds of the snow crunching beneath our feet.

The red barn had two large doors at the front. We walked around it to find a less conspicuous entrance. There was a single side door and a ladder at the back, which lead to a hayloft.

I pressed my ear to the side door and heard muffled voices farther into the barn. Cautiously cracking it open, I peeped in. Soft light illuminated a doorframe at the end of a dark hall.

We slipped into the barn and crept between rows of empty stables. Crouching, I gazed around the doorless frame. Jesse stood beside me, looking in from above my head.

I silenced my gasp with my hand over my mouth.

Candles flickered around the large room. Halos created by a thick fog of incense smoke surrounded their flames. The eerie light made the deep crimson paint on the floor look black. Bent over a stone altar, Leo grunted as Fjolnir fucked him with deep, hard thrusts. Though Leo's face was slack with pleasure, Fjolnir's was scrunched in concentration.

My stomach turned at the sight of his mouth flattened into a cruel line, his hard, blue eyes, and his blond hair plastered to his forehead with sweat.

Raven stood outside the circle with his arms spread wide, chanting.

"What am I watching?" I whispered to Jesse.

He bent down to murmur in my ear. "Raven is directing the magical energy being raised by Fjolnir and Leo back into Fjolnir."

"What'll happen next?"

"Presumably, he'll bleed Leo at the climax when a burst of magical energy is released. I don't know a lot about this, you know. This isn't my kind of magic."

I drew the gun from my pocket and looked around to devise a plan. Just as I was eyeing an oil can, Fjolnir grabbed a knife from the altar.

Without a thought, I stepped out and raised my revolver at him.

"Drop the knife, Cy...or do you prefer Fjolnir these days?"

Cy and his army buddy froze with their eyes wide. Leo slumped onto the altar, disoriented and unaware of what was happening. Cy dropped the knife, and it clattered onto the altar.

His face flushed. "Anna..." he whispered, one hand touching a murky white crystal hanging on a cord around his neck.

"Don't say my name. I don't want to hear it on your lips. Step away from Leo."

He slid out of Leo, whose moan of pleasure had a chilling effect in the contrasting scene, and took a step back with raised hands.

As I paused to think of how best to approach Leo, Victor flicked his wrist at me. My gun flew out of my hands. Before I could move to recover it, Victor had me by the throat from behind.

Jesse, who'd rushed out when I was disarmed, froze and cursed under his breath. Cy slowly reclaimed his knife and smiled.

"Don't move," Victor warned. "I may have transferred most of the power to Fjolnir, but I still have enough to kill you."

His tone said he was pleased to finally have a reason to end my life. Recalling the cold stares he'd given me after he and Cy had returned from the war, I stiffened in his arms.

"Bring her here, Raven," Fjolnir instructed.

"Why?" Victor asked, confused. "Let's just kill them both and get out of here."

"There's no need for that. Just hand her over, and I'll deal with her."

Raven took a step back, dragging me with him. "Are you... protecting her?" Jealousy tainted his voice.

Fjolnir didn't respond.

"Do you still have feelings for her?" Raven accused.

I saw a flicker of Cy in Fjolnir's eyes when our gazes

met. Unfortunately, Raven must've seen it too because he growled in my ear between clenched teeth.

"Problem easily solved," he whispered.

He began chanting words of magic, and his hand on my neck grew hot. Just as I opened my mouth to release a soundless scream, a loud bang echoed through the barn. The heat on my throat disappeared as Victor fell to the ground, a neat bullet hole between his wide, black eyes.

In the hayloft, Jack lowered his rifle to reload. Like my revolver, the rifle flew from his grasp. We all looked at Fjolnir, who held his reclaimed knife to a still-dazed Leo.

He clicked his tongue in irritation. "Damn it, Jack. Do you know how long it'll take to find another witch to help me realize my destiny? Get down here."

Jack slowly descended the hayloft and came to my side.

"Let Leo go. It's over," I demanded of Fjolnir.

Cy met my eyes, pleading for me to understand.

I shook my head. "I can't believe you'd do this."

"You don't understand," he defended.

"Oh, I think I got most of it. Faking your own death? Using love spells to lure in, rape, and murder witches so you can steal their magic and become one? I think that about covers it."

"Magic doesn't just belong to witches. Humans can use it."

"At what cost?"

"Everything has a price. Remember the hanged man? Knowledge through sacrifice. The fortune teller told me I was an achiever of the impossible. And look! I'm turning my human soul into a witch's soul. Other witches can't even tell the difference anymore. And now that I have a high priest, I can raise enough power to convert my soul forever."

"You've certainly achieved madness."

He frowned at my assessment then smiled like he had a brilliant idea. "It seems I've run into a minor setback, but this could be a blessing. Now, I can have you and achieve my dream. Come to me, Caill."

Jack grabbed my hand.

Fjolnir's lip curled in distaste.

"I'm sorry," I told Jack. I squeezed his fingers before letting go of his hand. "I'll come to you if you release Leo unharmed."

"Agreed." Fjolnir smiled and let Leo drop to the floor at his feet.

"I've never stopped loving you," Cy declared.

"Yeah? I thought you'd developed a taste for men." I took a small step toward him, the knife in my garter heavy with purpose.

"A means to an end," he explained, brushing off my comment. "I still remember how you feel and taste. It was such a difficult decision: the choice between you and my destiny. It was agony thinking about how I'd hurt you, but I knew you'd want me to be happy."

Cy's sparkling blue eyes smiled at me as I took another step closer. "I knew you'd always be my girl."

I heard Jack sniff hard, and my eyes flicked to his over my shoulder.

"That's enough, Cy, or whatever you call yourself now," Jack demanded, closing the short distance between us and grabbing my hand again.

I gasped, my sharp intake of breath loud in my ears.

"I'm not letting you go through with this," he murmured to me.

My heart swelled in my chest, warm and radiant, and my brain scrambled to adjust my plan.

Fjolnir clicked his tongue. "What is the meaning of this?"

"You knew," Jack accused. "You always knew how I felt about Anna, and still you took her for yourself."

"She loved me, Jack. She didn't even see you."

My face flushed at Jack's reminder, and I recalled Cy's reaction to my confession of love. "I should've listened to you, Cy," I told him as he smiled confidently.

As he searched my eyes for what used to be his, he asked, "You still love me. Don't you, Anna?"

"I should've always known Jack is my soulmate."

His eyes widened then squinted in rage. He growled, "Then be reunited in the Otherworld." His words of magic that followed raised the hair on my neck and arms like an electrical storm. As he held out his palm toward us, a pulse of energy erupted from him.

Seeing his purpose, Jack shoved me away, taking the brunt of the strike as the aftershock slammed Jesse and me into the wall. Blinking hard, I cleared my vision, focusing on Jack's limp form on the floor.

"Jack!" My own scream sounded far away as I stumbled toward him. I rolled him onto his back, placing his head in my lap.

"Anna," he breathed, weakly meeting my eyes.

Fjolnir clicked his tongue again. "That should have killed you," he muttered. "But there are easier ways."

He strode with purpose toward Jack's rifle on the floor.

Bang! Bang! Bang! Shots rang through the candlelit barn, having no effect on the steady flames. Fjolnir collapsed, sputtering as blood welled from multiple holes in his chest. Jesse lowered my revolver.

"He's right," Jesse commented, examining my weapon. "Human weapons are much more effective." Jesse approached him. "You just had to try to kill her. Didn't you? But if you hurt her, then you hurt me. We are bound, you see. And that little surge might have ended your human friend, but our blood oath puts her under my magic's protection." Jesse shook his head. "Achiever of the impossible," he scoffed. "You ought not to have meddled in the affairs of witches. Perhaps you will make better decisions in your next life."

Jesse's advice was the last thing Cy heard as his blood painted over the dried lines of the magic circle on the barn floor.

Jack's cold fingertips reached up and gently stroked the burns Victor had left on my throat, pulling my full attention back to him. "Anna, you're hurt," he whispered.

"Don't worry about me, Jack. I'm fine. It's you I'm concerned about. Can you move? Jesse and I are going to get you help. All right?"

"He's not going to make it. Fjolnir was right. You shouldn't have survived it," Jesse murmured, standing over us.

"What are you saying? Of course he's going to make it! We're fine." My voice cracked and gave out as my mouth went dry.

"He took most of it, and our blood oath protected you from the rest. If not for all that, you'd both be dying."

"He's not dying," I whispered.

"Anna," Jack called, pulling me from my argument with Jesse. "Anna, listen."

My eyes stung at the acceptance in his voice. "Jack, no. I love you."

He smiled sadly. "I've waited so long to hear you say that."

"And I will keep saying it, so don't go."

He touched the tears that streamed down my face. "Anna, I've always loved you, and I always will. Don't make the same mistakes you made after Cy. I don't want you to suffer. Be happy. I'll wait for you."

"I can't promise you that," I moaned.

"Yes, you can. I'm trusting you to take care of the woman I've loved all my life," he charged me.

I nodded, knowing the words wouldn't come out.

"Tell your father I will keep my promise to love and protect you from the other side."

A sob escaped my trembling lips.

"You will always be mine and I yours," he asserted.

I sealed his lips with mine. I tried to pour every missed moment where we should've been together into that kiss, and he accepted it all with equal passion.

"I love you, Jack."

He smiled, and his eyes dimmed.

ONE YEAR LATER

JESSE

A nna's eyes shined feverishly in the flickering light of the candles spread out around the motel room. The strong scent of incense filled my nose as I tried to steady my ragged breath enough to speak the words of magic. The energy we raised welled up inside me with a heat that spread to my limbs.

As she threw her head back in a shout of pleasure, I whispered the spell, pumping inside her. Spent from the effort, it wasn't difficult for me to step aside in my mind and allow him to take control of my body.

"Anna," he whispered, using my mouth to frown.

"Jack?" Her glazed eyes turned anxious, searching my gaze for the spirit of her soulmate. "How long do we have?"

"Not long," he answered. "I can already feel the other side pulling me back."

"Is it painful?"

He nodded my head. "Anna, you have to stop this. I told you I don't want you to suffer."

Her face steeled in the same nonnegotiable expression she wore when I made similar arguments. "I have to. The world is empty and dark. You were the only thing I was living for. And now, I have nothing. This is how I will keep going."

My heart panged, and I hoped Jack didn't feel that her comment had hurt me.

"So this is your life now? Performing sex magic with Jesse for a few short moments with me?"

Her eyes glistened with unshed tears, but her decision was resolute. "I'll do what I must, whatever I can to see you until we're together again."

He raised my hand to her cheek, his grief joining my own to double the ache in my chest. She didn't pull away from his comforting touch.

My muscles tensed, and I hissed as the anguish increased. I gasped for breath, my lungs squeezing, when Jack's soul was ripped from my body, back to where he belonged.

Her eyes dulled when she saw me return to myself. Frowning, she climbed off me. "The time he can stay is getting shorter," she said, heading to the bathroom to wash me off her.

This is all you get. She will never be more than this to you. Not in this life. Not in any life. "The longer he is in the Other-world, the more difficult it is for him to return to this life. And since the veil isn't thin, it takes more energy to call him here."

"Will he eventually not be able to come back?"

"Hard to say, but he should be able to continue to return as long as he doesn't move on to his next life."

There was a long pause. "He won't," she stated eventually. "He'll wait for me."

I sighed, knowing she was right.

She returned to the bedroom and started pulling on her clothes. I rose to dress and pack our things. I didn't have to tell her it was time for us to move on again. The Council of Covens had pardoned me from trying to cheat Leo because I'd handled Fjolnir, but the coppers were not so forgiving when a witch killed a human. Still, she had some unreasonable drive to take cases and help people where she could. And now she dragged me into it, as if avoiding the coppers wasn't hard enough.

Our blood oath may have been what kept her with me at first, but I knew as soon as I recovered, she would want to channel him again. Watching her from the corner of my eye, I smiled bitterly to myself. *You played your part too well, Jesse. Pull her in; push her away. If you'd just been honest, maybe you would have had a chance. Yeah, who are you kidding, pal? She has a soulmate, and she knows he's not you. She can't see that we are really the same: lost and broken. We will either save or destroy one another.*

ALSO BY D. LIEBER

Conjuring Zephyr

The Exiled Otherkin

Intended Bondmates

ABOUT THE AUTHOR

D. writes stories she wants to read. Her love of the worlds of fiction led her to earn a Bachelor's in English from Wright State University.

When she isn't reading or writing, she's probably hiking, crafting, watching anime, Korean television, Bollywood, or old movies. She may also be getting her geek on while planning her next steampunk cosplay with friends.

She lives in Wisconsin with her husband (John) and cats (Yin and Nox).

Links

    Website: www.dlieber.com
    Facebook: www.facebook.com/dlieberwriting
    Twitter: www.twitter.com/AuthorDLieber
    Instagram: www.instagram.com/dlieberwriting
    Pinterest: www.pinterest.com/dlieberwriting/
    Goodreads: www.goodreads.com/dlieberwriting

CPSIA information can be obtained
at www.ICGtesting.com
Printed in the USA
FSHW010202160719
60039FS